AMERICA REBOOTED

Phil Emmert

Published in the USA by thewordverve inc. (www.thewordverve.com)

eBook ISBN: 978-1-941251-77-5
Paperback ISBN: 978-1-941251-78-2

Library of Congress Control Number: 2016953723

America Rebooted
A Book with Verve by thewordverve inc.

Cover and interior design by Robin Krauss
www.bookformatters.com

eBook formatting by Bob Houston
facebook.com/eBookFormatting

PROLOGUE

Was this a horrible nightmare or had America actually been brutally attacked by a country that had threatened her for years? How could it be? How could America have been so naive to enter into an agreement with a nation that was never known to tell the truth? What had happened?

While all eyes were on China and Russia, North Korea had pulled a bait-and-switch scam. They had shown the world failed missile tests. Meanwhile, they had developed a ballistics missile that was virtually invisible to radar once it was launched.

They had manufactured hundreds of these missiles, and had secretly sold and shipped them, labeled as farm implements, to Iran. Iran had added both nuclear and conventional blockbuster warheads loaded with poison gas that had not been used since World War I. They had cunningly concealed them in silos around their vast desert. These weapons had been assembled right under the noses of the United Nations inspectors. Of course, these inspectors were a party to the devious scheme.

Follow the riveting account of a Christian family far from home, when a catastrophic, paralyzing attack strikes the continental United States. Jerry and April Hunt, along with their two preteen sons, survive and, with God's help, rescue others along the way. The nation is all but destroyed. Yet she rises from the ashes and becomes stronger than ever, by learning from the mistakes of the past.

ONE

Under a sky the color of amber, the slender teenager rolled over, opened his eyes, and looked up. He had seen a flash and felt a blast of heat that had knocked him off of his dirt bike. He had no idea how long he had been on the ground. The Kawasaki was lying on its side, still running at an idle with the rear wheel revolving slowly. Finally, when his head cleared, he stood the bike on its wheels and headed northwest on a paved road. He kept searching through eyes blurred with tears, but the skyline of St. Louis had disappeared. It was gone. A thick column of a strange golden haze hung over the area where the high-rises and office buildings should have been. He was terrified because his folks worked there in the city.

By the time the first bomb had exploded over New York City, so-called lone-wolf ISIS sympathizers and sleeper cells were carrying out individual attacks on smaller cities, power stations, and bridges with suitcase bombs by the dozens. The devices in the cities were often loaded with mustard and other chemical gases that had long ago been outlawed by the Geneva Convention. However, outlaws and outlaw nations do not obey laws.

Chicago, Los Angeles, Miami, Cincinnati, New Orleans, Seattle, and dozens of other cities were hit. Military bases in several states were also annihilated with these warheads. Only very rural areas had escaped destruction.

Survivors immediately reached for their cell phones, but it was no use. The only communication towers left were not powered. Technology seemed to be of no use when it was needed the most.

The country had so depended upon wireless communication that it was now in a comatose state. These strikes had been coordinated with a huge cyber attack just minutes before the missiles began to hit their targets. There were only very few small power grids operational in the whole continental United States. Bridges that crossed major rivers had been destroyed or were so severely damaged they could not be used.

How had Homeland Security missed these planned attacks? Obviously, there were government traitors who had helped coordinate these strikes. These collaborators had slipped into vital positions over the years and had waited patiently until this precise moment. Democracy and freedom were under severe assault.

Paralyzed was one of many words that came to the minds of so many survivors. Paralyzed, horrified, terrified . . . the nation was in a state of shock.

Martial Law had been declared, but few people knew about it for lack of communication. Television and radio stations were off the air. The attack was not designed to completely wipe out these large cities, but to leave as many injured, maimed, and burned survivors as possible—people who would need medical care for a long time and would experience a slow death. The bulk of the population would be disabled and defeated.

Meanwhile, in the sparsely populated areas of the country, no one was sure what had happened. Because of this uncertainty, there was impending dread in most of the towns and villages that were left intact.

TWO

Jerry Hunt had been on a camping vacation with his wife April and their two sons in Colorado. Lonnie, whom they called Lon, was twelve, and Jon was ten. Jerry and his family had motored way out west from Greensboro, North Carolina, and had just started the return trip. Jerry was due to be back at work at his dad's plumbing and electrical business in a couple of days.

When Jerry stopped for gas, he noticed the price had spiked more than double since he'd last filled up. He entered the station to question the sudden change in pricing.

The owner—a man who looked to be in his seventies—said he didn't know what had happened, but all communication was lost from coast to coast. The electricity was out but his gas pumps were operational, as they were powered by a generator. Bad weather in that part of the country often knocked out the electricity, so the old man was ready for it. As they discussed what had happened, they surmised it had to be some sort of disaster. But was it manmade or natural? Jerry pointed out the strange color of the sky and asked if it was common at this time of year in that part of the country.

The old man replied, "No sir, something has obviously polluted the atmosphere." His guesses were that it was a huge volcano eruption or worse—a nuclear attack. The air was noticeably cooler now and little bits of something that looked like grains of sand had started falling from the sky.

Jerry bought as much gas as the man would sell him, which was thirty gallons. He filled the GMC Yukon and two five-gallon gas cans. He also bought all the bottled water and canned goods he could stuff into his sport utility vehicle.

He had always tried to be prepared for the unexpected. He had extra cash and several gold coins worth almost two thousand dollars in a money belt he wore strapped around his waist.

Jerry instructed his wife and children to put on the ponchos they had brought on their camping trip and to keep the windows closed on the Yukon. If the particles falling from the sky were radioactive or toxic, the family would be somewhat protected.

He drove east on US 52 toward Kansas. He had traveled but a few miles when he met a caravan of about twenty vehicles heading west. He flagged one of them down; the news was that no one could get east of the Mississippi River. All bridges were down or deemed to be unsafe. The rumor was that it had been a massive, unprovoked attack on the country. A ham radio operator in the mountains of upper New York had supposedly verified this. The caravan of cars and trucks were heading for Mexico.

Jerry was a former SEAL, and his mind was working overtime. He parked on the side of the road and did some calculating. His best bet for survival was to go deep into the wilderness. Jerry was a little old-fashioned in terms of technology, and now he was glad. The GPS was useless. However, he had a road atlas which he always kept in the spare tire compartment. His SEAL training had taught him that in cases of Murphy's Law, he should always have contingency plans.

No one can save me and my family but me, he thought, then quickly added, And you, Lord. Just you and me, Lord. After Jerry had completed two tours in Iraq and one in Afghanistan, he had become a Christian. He knew he had survived by the grace of God and would never forget that fact.

Jerry found what looked like a logging road that made a steep climb up a mountain. He looked ahead, and then into the rearview mirror; no one was in sight. He quickly turned off the highway and stopped. Taking a whiskbroom from the glove box, he erased his tire tracks. From the highway, no one could tell a vehicle had turned onto the dirt road. The Yukon slowly made the climb, out of sight of the main road, and around a bend. He had driven a mile or so when he found a clearing off to the right, about twenty-five yards through some small underbrush. He told the boys to straighten up the bushes he had driven over. From the dirt road, it would appear that no one had ever come through there.

He began to plan the steps they would take for survival. He figured if this disaster were as large as he suspected, other survivors would be his worst enemy. Most people were not prepared for such a disaster. They would be looking for others to victimize and rob.

Jerry had a couple of weapons in the Yukon—a 9mm Glock and a short-barreled .223 Colt Expanse M4 rifle. He had a sufficient number of rounds and was skilled with both weapons.

They would need to conserve as much of their supplies as possible. He had no idea how long they would need to be self-sufficient. They would try to eat one good meal a day and then just snacks, such as crackers, dried fruit, and trail mix the rest of the time.

April prepared a meal that afternoon of Spam, fruit cocktail, and flat bread fried in an iron skillet. She often made this bread when they were camping. The bread was tough and chewy, but filling.

It was eerily quiet when evening came. The darkness came early due to the heavy atmosphere. Everyone got into their sleeping bags. It was cooler than it had been on previous nights. Jerry was glad that his and April's sleeping bags could be zipped together for extra warmth. The comfort of their bodies next to each other didn't hurt either. He instructed the boys to do the same. Just before they fell to sleep, Jerry led the family in a prayer.

THREE

Arising before daylight, Jerry glanced at the luminous dial on his watch. It was 0435 hours. The first thing he did was what he had been doing every morning for over ten years. It was just him and Jesus in their morning conversation. Then he made some coffee on the camp stove and drank the strong mixture as he went over some plans in his head.

He didn't necessarily have—nor did he need—a destination at this time. He just needed to make sure he and his family survived. He would scout around on foot today and check the possibility for water and game. He thought perhaps he should really try to get farther off the beaten track.

After a breakfast of instant grits and the rest of the fruit cocktail from last night, the boys were put to the task of camouflaging the Yukon while Jerry dug a slit-trench latrine some ten yards away. He would break out the small tent only if it looked like rain. It was low to the ground and easy to disguise. In the meantime, they would sleep under the stars . . . except they hadn't seen any stars, or the sun, just the ominous amber-colored clouds.

Just before Jerry left the camp area, he remembered the toy walkie-talkies the boys had brought with them. They were battery-operated and had a range of almost a mile. He left one with April and took the other.

Jerry walked in the grade line of the road, leaving no footprints. He headed toward the north and had gone about two miles when he heard running water—a small brook. He shook his head in disgust. He had forgotten to bring an empty water bottle with him. He made a mental note to shape up and make a list. He could not afford to make even little mistakes like this.

He noted a few squirrels scurrying about and signs of rabbits. Near the brook, he had also seen some deer tracks. Perhaps he would have the boys make some snares for the small game, so they could have some fresh meat a night or two. He traveled on about two more miles but saw nothing else remarkable before retracing his steps back to the campsite.

As he got close to the camp, he called April on the walkie-talkie to let her know he was approaching. Everything was fine with the family, April reported. His excursion had lasted only four hours. Once he arrived, he filled everyone in on what he had found—it was important to keep everyone informed.

Then it dawned on Jerry that he had not really taken

a good look at his family lately. He got up and walked over to April, took her hand, and lifted her to her feet. He hugged her to his chest and planted a firm kiss on her lips. He then just held her at arms length and looked at her as if he had just seen her for the first time. She gave him a confused look. Jerry seldom did things like that, just to be doing them. She smiled and returned the kiss.

Now April could not be described as a beautiful lady, but she was attractive and had not lost her figure. With her long legs and slender frame, she could easily pass for a twenty-five-year-old. She had dark hair and the prettiest wide-set, brown eyes that had first caught Jerry's attention.

The boys sure do look a lot like her, Jerry thought. Their eyes and hair were the same as their mom's but their frame would be short and muscular, like Jerry's. As he surveyed his family, he was overwhelmed with pride. In this emergency situation they had not complained or whined. They had done everything he had asked. Perhaps he would take one of the boys with him next time he explored.

April was a very smart lady in her own right. She could handle an automobile or weapon as skillfully as any man he had ever seen. Her training started early as a farm girl in rural Tennessee. Her parents had both died in an auto accident during her senior year of high school. With the support of friends and family, she managed to finish out the school year and graduate. She then joined the Marines.

She had stayed in the service for two hitches, serving as a truck driver, transporting water, supplies, and gasoline in Iraq.

That was where she and Jerry had first met.

They had stayed in touch and finally got married after he left the service. They both loved the same things— mostly outdoor things. This camping trip was one of many they had taken since the boys were very small.

FOUR

The sky was almost as amber as the day before, and there was a strange odor in the air. It smelled like an overstuffed chair that they had once tried to burn. The grainy sand was still coming down but not as much as yesterday. Near as Jerry could tell, they were just a few miles north of Cheyenne Wells. Kansas was to the east and Nebraska was just about due north.

Jerry noticed the birds were singing today. He heard the chirping of a cardinal and the twitter of a wren. Somewhere in the distance, a blue jay was raising a ruckus and a woodpecker was working on a tree. Jerry was glad to hear the birds, for it meant the air was not toxic, even though it was polluted.

After a breakfast of coffee, flatbread and honey, and a handful of nuts, Jerry said, "Lon, I want you to go with me today."

Lon jumped at the chance to be with his dad. He was ready to go in about two minutes. Jerry told him to double-check and make sure they had everything they needed to take the excursion into the unknown. And this time Jerry didn't forget the empty water bottles.

Jerry strapped on his Glock. He put a hatchet, hunting knife, compass, and a cigarette lighter in a backpack. They also took two round cakes of flatbread and a can of pears with them.

They walked as quickly as possible along the grade line and only stepped into the road on occasion. They paused from time to time to listen for any manmade sounds. After about five miles, they found a downed tree just off the road. Taking a seat, they drank some water and rested for a moment in the quiet. They then walked in a wide circle, looking for a camping area that might be better suited for hiding them from human eyes. Ultimately, Jerry decided that, for the time being, he still liked their current campsite the best. But he would keep looking.

On the walk back, they filled the four empty water bottles from the brook he had found the prior day. They arrived back at the camp in the middle of the afternoon. Jerry told them all he was very proud of them. He said, "You guys are the best squad I have ever led." The boys beamed with pride, and April gave him a big hug and a kiss right on the lips.

Jerry was not sure about the water they'd collected. It had no odor, and it was clear as crystal; but just to make sure, he dropped a chlorine tablet in each. He would ask

April to look around their stash for a larger container, and then they could dump all the water together. It would not take as many chlorine tablets that way. After the supper meal, Jerry shared with April and Jon what they had seen that day. He said they might find another campsite a little deeper in the woods. He noted that in two days they had not heard any motorized vehicles or aircraft.

Day 3, Another Move

Jerry decided to go it alone this time. He could travel faster by himself and explore more territory in a short period of time. Lon and Jon were disappointed. April was relieved. She really wanted both of her boys with her. Jerry gave instructions that one of the boys should serve as a lookout at all times so no one could surprise them. April set up a schedule; the boys would take turns an hour at a time just down the road from their campsite.

As he knew would be the case, Jerry traveled faster than he had the last two days. He walked briskly and figured he had walked ten miles by noon. He noticed the land off to the south began to rise before him. He walked into the woods on that side, and the land climbed sharply, almost like a cliff, when he had gone about two hundred yards from the road. He walked and climbed for another twenty-five yards and suddenly he felt a puff of cool air— almost like a fan was blowing out of the side of the hill.

He pulled some branches and vines away, and there was an opening into the side of the cliff—a natural cave. He had to get on his hands and knees to enter. With his service flashlight, he could see that it went pretty far back, perhaps thirty feet or so. Once inside, about five feet from the entrance, he could stand; the ceiling was at least fifteen feet high. Jerry smiled to himself; he had found the perfect campsite. A home away from home.

Jerry got on his knees in that cave and prayed to God. He thanked the Lord for leading him to this place, where his family would be safer. His eyes were rather blurry when he got off his knees. Tears of thanksgiving and joy flooded over him.

He carefully marked the place, noting everything about it in his mind, and then returned to his family. Jerry was almost to the camp when he glanced at his watch. It was 1800 hours. He heard a rustling in the brush, and a high-pitched voice said, "Halt, who goes there?" It was Jon. He then giggled and said, "It's okay, Daddy, come on in."

Jerry reported to the others what he had found. The boys were excited about the new campsite—apparently this one had become boring to them. April also seemed happy—they had no clue as to how long it would be before they saw North Carolina again. A cave would give far more protection than their tent. She fixed a nice meal of dried beef gravy over flatbread and some instant potatoes. A can of peaches and bottled water topped it off—a perfect celebratory meal.

Day 4

Jerry arose about 0500 hours. He had his morning prayer and a cup of coffee. He would wait until it was light to wake everyone. But by 0600 hours, everyone was awake anyway. They were all anxious to see their new home and to move in.

The plan was to load everything in the Yukon and drive as close to the cave as possible. They would carry everything they had to the cave, and when the SUV was empty, Jerry would drive it back to the original campsite and hide it. If they needed it in the future, they would know where to find it. But even more importantly, if it were discovered . . . well, it was not close to their new campsite, so it made no difference. He would also disable the vehicle by removing the fuel pump fuse; that way, it couldn't be easily stolen if it should be found.

It took them until the middle of the afternoon to get everything in the cave. Jerry then had the boys cover all the tracks that led to the cave. If they could get a rain shower or two, Jerry figured that after a week or so, it would be as if they hadn't ever been around.

He told the family that he would be spending the

night at the old campsite and returning to the cave in the morning. At the old site, he spent an hour camouflaging the vehicle and covering the tracks. He then curled up and spent the night in the back of the SUV.

Back at the cave, April was organizing their haul. This was definitely her forte, and she took it seriously.

By the time it was dark, everyone was very tired from the day's activities. April tucked the boys in and said a prayer for them and for Jerry. She felt very alone and just a little frightened. As she dozed off, she thought to herself, I am not as brave as Jerry thinks I am.

Day 5

Just before daylight, Jerry started walking on the dirt road, heading back to the cave. He paused when he thought he heard something. It sounded like machinery down on the highway. He had heard this sound before when he was in Iraq. It sounded like a military tank—the deep growl of a diesel engine and the clank of tracks on pavement. Then the sound grew fainter and was gone. His heart was in his throat. He didn't want anyone to know where they were, at least not until they knew exactly what was going on.

He raced on, walking as fast as he could. He arrived opposite the cave at about 1030 hours. He had made good time. Up the steep incline to the cave entrance, he thought to himself, Wow, it's hidden better than I thought. He missed the entrance by about ten yards, but then Lon whistled for him and waved.

"This is a good hiding place," Jerry said to April as he hugged her. She planted a huge, rough kiss on his mouth. With a boyish grin on his face, he said, "Maybe I need to stay away a little more often if you're going to greet me that way."

Jerry made a schedule for guard duty. Everyone would take a turn. He posted someone at the entrance of the cave during the daylight hours. They could, of course, do other things at the same time. They just needed to keep their eyes on the road and make sure everyone was alerted if someone approached. He devised a series of hand signals, so in case of an intruder, they could communicate silently. With security organized, he dug a narrow latrine just down the hill and instructed the boys about its proper use. "Always remember to cover your tracks," he said.

The boys had a couple of board games to occupy them. He and April read the Bible and played cards. Jerry wished he had some of his books from his library back home, but he knew wishing wasn't going to change anything. April had brought some knitting with her on their vacation, but she only had four balls of yarn.

Jerry knew from his experience in the military that boredom could become a real enemy. He would invent games and activities for the family if he could. He would also make sure everyone worked out every day. They all needed to stay fit and strong.

FIVE

ack in Missouri, a seventeen-year-old Ned Carney was making his way westward as fast as his dirt bike could safely carry him. His folks had been in St. Louis the day of the attack. He was sure they were dead. He had stopped by his home and put several cans of meat, fruit, and a change of clothes in a tote bag. He strapped it to his Kawasaki, along with two small, plastic cans of gasoline. At the last minute, he remembered the emergency money his mom always left in a sock drawer. He quickly counted it. It came to two hundred thirty-five dollars. Ned didn't have time to mourn for his family and friends in the city. His survival instinct had taken over.

Late on the second day, Ned glanced at the gas gauge and saw it was getting low. He dumped the cans of gasoline into the tank. He had gone for miles without seeing a house or a living soul. On the third day at about three o'clock in the afternoon, he saw a farmhouse and outbuildings in the distance. He left his bike a quarter of a mile down the road in a ditch. He sneaked closer to the house, where he saw an older man and woman on the porch. On the porch floor lay a black and white border collie with a litter of puppies.

The lady was lovingly fussing over the pups, who appeared to be near weaning age. Ned lay in the ditch, observing. There was an overhead gas tank in the barnyard. No way of telling if it had anything in it, or if it was gas or diesel.

He looked up at the sky, which was already darkening. Darkness came earlier now; he figured it was due to the change in atmosphere, whatever had happened. An oil lamp shined in the living room window. Ned dropped off to sleep. What seemed like hours later, he was startled awake, and it took a few seconds for him to remember he was lying in a ditch. There were no lights visible in the house. He looked at his watch with his small penlight. It was one o'clock in the morning. Off in the distance was a flash of lightning and, a few seconds later, the sound of thunder.

Ned opened a can of Vienna sausages and put three of them in his jacket pocket. He sneaked toward the barnyard. The mama dog came off the porch with a low growl in her throat. Ned spoke softly to her and extended a sausage. She wagged her tail and eagerly wolfed it down. As Ned made his way to the overhead tank, she followed him, expecting some more food. At the tank, he noticed the padlock was open. Either the tank was empty, or these folks were very trusting people.

Ned had the two gas cans tied to his waist. He opened one of them as he took the nozzle down and turned the valve. After pressing the lever, he took a whiff. Thankfully, it was gasoline. He quickly filled both cans, gave the dog another sausage, and then quietly retreated from the barnyard.

Back at the motorcycle, he filled the tank. Then he sneaked back to the barnyard where the mama dog and one little pup were waiting for him. He fed the hungry dog one more sausage and quickly pumped two more full cans of gas. He folded up a ten-dollar bill, weighed it down with the gas nozzle, and he was gone.

As he tied the gas cans on the bike, lightening flashed close by and a very loud peal of thunder sounded. Ned instantly felt a tug on his pant leg. It was the little black and white pup. He was shaking like a leaf, and his mama was not in sight. Ned didn't hesitate; he reached down, scooped up the pup, and hugged him to his cheek. He was rewarded with a wet tongue against his face. Without another thought, he stuffed the puppy inside his windbreaker.

Ned felt a little bad about taking the pup. He had never stolen anything in his life. But he needed some companionship. His folks had promised him a dog for years but never made good on their promise. Ned thought to himself, *Sometimes you have to take matters in your own hands.*

Several hours later, it still had not rained and he had outrun the threatening storm. Ned was pretty sure he was about to pass over the state line into Nebraska or Kansas, but he had not been this far west since he was a little child. He had no compass but was sure he was heading west/ northwest. However, he was traveling secondary roads, so he couldn't be absolutely sure. The traffic he had seen on the main roads was heavy. He didn't trust people at a time like this, so he had stayed on the less-traveled roads.

SIX

Day 6, Life at the Cave

The temperature never seemed to fluctuate much in the cave. Night or day, it was constant and not as damp as April had anticipated. "All the comforts of home except for tables, chairs, and beds," she said with a big grin on her face. Everyone laughed as Lon added, "Or electricity and TV."

At about 1200 hours, as they were snacking on some trail mix and water for their lunch, it began to rain. It was the first rain they had seen in several days. Jerry quickly rigged up some canvas to catch rainwater for bathing and washing clothes. He wanted to keep as much of the brook water for drinking, as he felt it was safer.

They sat in the shelter of the cozy cave and watched it rain. Very comforting, April thought. She and Jerry lay down and took a nice nap with the sound of rain just outside. The boys were playing monopoly and fussing over who owned what.

The rain stopped about 1730, and Jerry took the boys

outside to have a look around. The rain had erased any and all signs of human habitation in the area. The only way anyone could discover them now would be by pure accident.

The meals were getting a little boring. The flatbread was good to fill up on, but they actually needed some variety. Jerry found some old parachute cord he had put in his backpack. He and the boys unloaded the canned goods from the wooden box and carried the box outside with them. Down the hill a couple hundred feet, they set a trap. Using the cord and a stick to prop up one end of the box, they then ran the cord out until the box could just barely be seen through the brush.

If they wanted fresh meat, someone would need to stand guard. Underneath the box, they put a few nuts and a piece of flatbread with peanut butter on it. They had no idea what they might catch. That evening they caught nothing. At dark, Jerry brought the trap and the bait back to the cave.

Day 7, Primitive Worship

Jerry arose early and remembered it was Sunday. They had worshipped in a little church near Denver last Sunday. He had hoped to be in their home church by today. But he was determined that his family was going to remember the Lord and worship Jesus Christ regardless of where they were.

They ate a light breakfast of canned fruit, some nuts, and, of course, some flatbread. At 0900, Jerry called his family to worship. He said they might have to live like heathens, but they were going to worship like Christians.

Jerry read from Exodus about how the Israelites had fled from Egypt and God had fed them with manna and water. He told the boys, "God will provide. He always has, and he will again. We must have faith."

During the prayer time, April prayed, "Thank you, Lord, that we are all here together and are safe."

Jerry prayed that he would be a good father and husband, and then he said, "Lord, also make a preacher out of me so I can keep my family on the straight and narrow. In the name of Jesus, I pray. Amen."

The boys both said short prayers of thanksgiving for Momma and Daddy. Lon also thanked the Lord for a "nice dry place in this cave." Jon said, "Thank you, Lord, for flatbread and fruit. Amen."

Jerry told April, "You know we always have communion on Sunday. We don't have any grape juice or unleavened bread, but we have water and crackers." Jerry and April each broke off a piece of cracker and ate it. Then Jerry took a sip of the water and passed it to April, who also sipped.

Jerry said, "Lord, we eat and drink this in remembrance of you. And we are sorry, but this is the best we can do today." It was a simple but very spiritual service. They imagined it must have been much like the worship services found in the New Testament. They all sang a song that the congregation at their old church used to sing, "The Family of God."

I'm so glad I'm a part of the family of God,
I've been washed in the fountain, cleansed by His blood!
Joint heirs with Jesus as we travel this sod,
For I am part of the family, the family of God.

After setting the box trap and posting Lon to watch it, Jerry spent the afternoon planning what to do next. They had a comfortable, protected place to stay, but he really wanted to know what had happened and to perhaps get home . . . if home was still there.

A little after 1615 hours, Lon came running to the cave, shouting, "We got one, we got one! We got a rabbit!" Jerry went to the trap. Through the slats, he could see a medium-sized jackrabbit, which are larger than a cottontail, but a lot of bone too. He told Lon to go fetch the rifle. It would be quieter than the Glock, and not as messy. Through the slats, he could see the rabbit's head. Lon handed him the rifle, and he quickly dispatched the rabbit with one shot.

Jerry dressed it out and schooled the boys in the

process as he did so. After soaking the carcass in saltwater overnight, it would provide them one very different kind of meal. As it turned out, Mr. Jackrabbit was a little on the tough side, but with salt, pepper, and some hot sauce, he was pretty tasty.

SEVEN

Ned Carney motored west as much as possible, mostly on gravel roads. At least he hoped he was still heading west. He saw a country gas station up ahead. He could see a couple of cars in front and a group of men just standing around. He could not avoid other humans forever. He would take a chance. Dumping the last of the gas in the Kawasaki, he secured the empty cans on the back. He slowly approached the group of men at a low speed and kept a wary eye on them. They didn't look hostile, just a group of farmers banding together for safety.

As he made his approach, the men at the station were eyeing Ned just as intently. Ned wondered what they were thinking, like maybe he was one of those "lone-wolf" ISIS members. Several of the men had rifles or shotguns, and one or two had pistols strapped on.

Ned stopped his bike about thirty feet away and opened his jacket, exposing only a small pup. As he spoke to them, he held his hands out to show he was unarmed and meant no harm. One of the men spoke to him in a Midwestern drawl. "Howdy, friend, where you from and where are you heading?" Ned introduced himself and told them all he knew. They seemed sincerely sorry about his parents. But they were thankful for the information. This was more than they had known before.

They invited him to rest a spell. He asked them if they had any gas they could sell him. They had gasoline in the large storage tank behind the station, but so far, they had not figured out how to pump it. The owner of the station, which was actually a combination gas station and country store, said they were working on getting a generator set up. But they had to be careful how they connected it— didn't want to cause an explosion. One of the men in the community who was an electrician was on his way.

Ned parked his bike next to the station and took a seat on an old bus seat out front. One of the men laughed and said it was the local "liar's bench." Ned sat, petted his little pup, hugged him to his cheek, and fed him a Vienna sausage. He had been trying to think of an impressive name for his pup. He remembered from his literature class that Thor was the name of the mythical Greek god of thunder. Since it was thunder that had scared the little guy, he decided to name him Thor. When Ned took the pup's head in his hands, looked him in the eyes, and said, "Your name is Thor," the pup's ears shot up and he licked Ned right in the face. Thor seemed to like his new name.

After the electrician showed up, the pumps were pumping gas in about an hour. Ned filled the Kawasaki as well as one gas can, and purchased two bottles of water—

all at an elevated price. He thought to himself that he needed to conserve his money, because food, water, and gas were just going to get more expensive. The men at the station said if he just stayed the way he was going, he would soon be in Colorado.

Ned and his new charge spent the night on the old bus seat at the station. He shared his breakfast of canned tuna, crackers, and half a cup of water with Thor. He was on his way before anyone arrived at the station the next morning.

EIGHT

Day 8

Jerry told April they could not just stay hunkered down like frightened animals and wait things out. He needed to see if he could gather some information. His plan was to walk back to the SUV and drive north to see if there were any villages not shown on the atlas. He told April he might be gone for two or three days. She was not happy about it, and said, "Why can't we all go with you?"

He replied firmly, "No, I will not endanger you and the boys." April wrinkled her nose, but didn't argue. "A military unit can only have one leader in charge."

She sarcastically saluted him and said, "Yes sir." Then she kissed him on the cheek and hugged him for a full thirty seconds. She didn't want to let go of him, and she told him so—his muscular frame made her feel secure.

Day 9, Gathering Information

Jerry left the cave camp the next morning with enough food and water for three days. He strapped on his Glock and left the rifle with April. He also reminded the boys of their duties while he was gone. They held a prayer circle just outside the cave and said their goodbyes. Then he disappeared in the underbrush.

Jerry walked briskly and was back at the SUV within two hours. It was exactly as he had left it. After inserting the fuel pump fuse, the Yukon fired right up. He carefully eased the vehicle the twenty-five yards to the road. Down the mountain for a mile and a half, he then turned right and drove north.

He set the trip meter so he would know how far he had traveled. He passed three vehicles that appeared to have been abandoned. He supposed they were out of gas and maybe the folks had caught rides with others. But he really didn't know. He was in northern Colorado, and there were few communities.

After he had driven fifteen miles, he came to a crossroad with a little store on one corner and a cluster of houses along one road. There were two cars parked near the store. Jerry stopped. He could see that someone was inside the store, looking out the window at him. He decided to leave the Glock in the vehicle, but he locked the car as he exited.

In the store were a middle-aged man and woman behind the counter and an old man sitting on a stool beside an almost-empty candy case. Jerry greeted them, and they did the same but eyed him with suspicion. He introduced himself and assured them he meant them no harm. They seemed to relax a little.

The man behind the counter stepped out, shook Jerry's hand, and said his name was Frank Shockley and his wife's name was Thelma. Jerry noted Frank was wearing a long-barreled .357 Magnum Smith & Wesson on his hip. It was just like Dirty Harry's weapon.

Frank told Jerry the same thing he had heard on that first day. There had been an attack on the United States that had pretty much disabled the country. Some ham radio operators had been in contact and that was about all the information they had. Power was down and microwave towers were disabled.

Martial law had been declared, but the local sheriff had given his permission for his county's residents to arm themselves. The federal government had been unable to protect them, but as he said, "By God we will not be helpless!" Jerry smiled and thought, Now there is a man after my own heart.

Jerry asked if they had seen any military vehicles around. Yes, a couple of tanks and a troop carrier with about two dozen men had come through a few days back. They stopped and bought some candy and drinks. They were the ones who had informed them that martial law was in effect. The president, vice president, and many members of Congress were believed dead—a nuclear warhead had made a direct hit on Washington, DC.

The Speaker of the House of Representatives, Paul Ryan, had been in his hometown in Wisconsin for the funeral of a family member at the time of the attack and had not been injured. He had been sworn in by a federal judge from his home district, and was now the president of the United States.

Military units from the National Guard were sent to secure the state line. They were checking the IDs of people who were coming into the state, looking for anyone who might be ISIS or other terrorist faction members. And yes, they were profiling those who looked Middle Eastern or had Arabic-sounding names. Political correctness didn't seem all that important in the face of recent events.

Jerry thanked the Shockleys for the information and wished them well. Back on the road, he continued to drive north. Just outside a town named Hale, where the road crosses into Kansas, there was a roadblock. The National Guardsmen were allowing traffic going east to go through without stopping. Westbound was backed up as the Guardsmen checked IDs. Jerry turned around and parked on the other side of the road. He sure didn't want to cross into Kansas and not be able to get back to his family.

He noticed a young man on a dirt bike being detained and harassed. The boy didn't look to be more than sixteen or seventeen. He looked scared. The guard examined his cycle and everything on it. As the boy opened his windbreaker, a little furry head with a black nose and two bright eyes appeared. A puppy.

Jerry noted that the boy had one can of gasoline strapped to the bike, and he talked the men into letting him dump the gas into his tank. The other can was already empty, so he just left both of them on the side of the road.

They finally stepped aside and let the boy continue on his way. As he started to pass by, Jerry stepped into the road and stopped him. He told the boy he meant him no harm and introduced himself. At this, the boy smiled and said his name was Ned Carney and he had driven off and on for nine days—all the way from St. Louis. Ned told Jerry his story and was almost in tears by the time he finished.

Jerry took Ned's hand in his and said, "You're going to be all right." As he said these words, a voice in Jerry's head whispered, "Take him with you." Jerry had learned over the last few years not to ignore that voice. And he didn't. Out of the clear blue, he said, "Son, why don't you come with me? My family and I are living in a cave just south of here, thirty miles or so. It's safe and fairly comfortable."

Jerry could tell Ned was taken aback by the invitation and hoped the boy would realize the sincerity of the offer. Ned paused a minute and said, "Truth is, I have no real destination in mind. I think I'll take you up on that offer, but my pup has to go with me."

Smiling, Jerry said, "Not a problem, son."

The bike was a medium-sized, off-road Kawasaki, and by putting all the seats down in the Yukon, they were able to fit the bike in the back.

Jerry had hoped to do a little more exploring, but he could see it might be futile at this time. Besides, he just wanted to get back to his family. He drove back to the original campsite, making sure no one had seen him turn onto the mountain road. He and Ned covered the tracks and camouflaged the vehicle. They unloaded the Kawasaki, and since it was almost dark, they spent the night in the Yukon.

The next morning, Jerry disabled the vehicle, and they pushed the Kawasaki to the dirt road. It would really be loaded down, but they got on the bike and off they went in the direction of the cave camp.

They had to stop a couple of times to rest and let Thor relieve himself. However, they were close to the camp by 0700 hours. Jerry wanted to make sure April didn't take a shot at them, so he began to call to her from the road. "Hello, hello, April. Hello, Lon . . . Jon . . . April. Hello!"

He had called out like this a couple of times when he saw the brush moving, and April peeked out with the .223 in her hands. She had a big smile on her face until she saw Jerry wasn't alone. A puzzled look took over her expression.

"It's all right, sweetheart; he is a friend. And he's all alone in this world."

Jerry made the introductions and let Ned tell his story. As soon as she heard that his parents were likely dead, April put her arms around him and kissed him on the cheek. Ned began to sob, and Thor began to whimper. It was the first time Ned had actually openly wept in all this time.

This was another mouth to feed, but it was also another resource. Jerry had Ned ride the dirt bike up to the cave, where they dragged it inside for safe keeping.

Ned assured the family that his pup would not require any additional food from them. He would share whatever they gave him with Thor. Lon and Jon fell in love with Thor immediately. Ned easily became a part of the family routine, as if he had known them all his life. He played Monopoly with the boys and did his part of the daily chores. His lot was to search out and bring in loads of firewood.

NINE

Day 31

While Jerry had been gone, April made a discovery that would come in handy when winter arrived. She had heated some water just inside the entrance to the front of the cave with a wood fire.

She wanted to take a bath and didn't want to waste the cooking gas to heat bathwater. She thought the smoke would be drawn from the entrance to the outside. Instead, the smoke drifted to the ceiling of the large room and toward the back of the cave and disappeared up a small hole in the ceiling. It was drawing like a chimney.

After she had taken her bath and washed some clothes, she built another larger fire at the back wall of the cave, right underneath the hole. It worked like a charm. She'd thought, Why, this is like living inside a big fireplace.

They would later discover that it was quite a blessing.

Every day Ned, Lon, Jon, and Thor made an excursion into the forest and picked up as much downed firewood that they could carry. They made two piles, which they separated by size—kindling and smaller pieces in one pile and larger pieces in the other. They carefully covered the wood so it looked natural. Once while they were looking for firewood, they also dragged two larger logs to the cave, and after much struggle and help from Jerry, they were able to push and pull them into the cave. They now had something to sit on other than just the dirt and stone floor.

When April had proudly pointed out her discovery of their "chimney," Jerry examined the hole where the smoke exited the cave. It was about the size of an eight-inch stovepipe. Since he didn't have a stovepipe, he fashioned one out of a dead log. It took him almost a week to hollow it out with his hunting knife and a sharpened camp spoon. The log was about four feet long. He stuck it in the hole and wedged it tight with some sticks and rocks. It stuck up about three feet above the ground. When the snow came, they would have to make sure this opening was clear.

The family had become pretty lax about checking the road for any traffic, because they had seen no one on it since they moved in. But just to be on the safe side, they would burn no wood in the daytime until it got really cold.

The days came and went without incident. Every morning Jerry had everyone up at 0700 hours. He had them doing their exercises and running in place for at least twenty minutes. There were occasional moans some mornings, but they were actually quite a disciplined group.

Ned didn't have a sleeping bag, so April and Jerry took two ponchos and two extra blankets and made him one. It was not very soft, but after Ned collected some pine needles and put them under the whole thing, he said it felt like a feather mattress to him.

***

Day 48

Late in the day, Jerry was reading his Bible near the front of the cave. Thor began to whimper and ran to the entrance of the cave. Then Jerry's ears picked up a sound that made his heart skip. He held up his hand and told everyone to be quiet. They all held their breath and listened. Ned grabbed hold of Thor and kept him quiet.

It was closer now—the sound of a tracked vehicle. It sounded like a tank to him. Jerry crept on his stomach to the front of the cave. Peeking through the brush, he saw nothing, but the sound was louder now. Jerry could tell the diesel engine had a supercharger on it and was traveling at a fast pace. Then it came into view. It was an M2 Bradley tank, followed by two lightly-armored personnel carriers. They roared on past the cave and were soon out of sight. Finally, it was quiet again.

Jerry had not been east on the road below, so he had no idea where it led. He made a mental note to find out very soon.

Jerry took April aside and told her he was going to

explore farther east on Monday. Tomorrow, they would simply rest and worship God.

Sunday dawned on the cool side, and the sky threatened rain or snow. And for the first time, Jerry noted the sky had almost lost its amber tint.

He had everyone up by 0800 on Sunday. They skipped the exercise regimen, and as a special treat, April prepared pancakes. She had enough flour for several more meals, and she had made syrup from sugar and water with a little Karo syrup added. A large can of sliced peaches and coffee completed the meal.

At 0900 hours, Jerry called the family to worship. They sang some songs, and when they couldn't remember the words, Jon made up some lyrics—he was the more mischievious of the two boys and was always making up rhymes. The boys wanted to read the scripture, and Jerry asked April to lead them in prayer.

Ned was a little hesitant about the worship service that took place every Sunday. But since he was a guest, and grateful for it, he went along with the routine. But he never participated. He could only remember going to church very few times and had never really understood the preacher. This group, however, made up a rather unique congregation. A rough-bearded man, who must have looked a little like John the Baptist, was leading the service. One attractive lady, a teenage boy, two preteen boys, and a pup sitting with his head cocked to one side, as if he were asking a question, completed the picture.

Jerry delivered a short homily from Romans 12:1-3. Ned confessed later that it was the first lesson he'd ever understood from the Bible. To end the service, Jerry and April had a communion service with crackers and water as the emblems. Ned had been puzzled about communion on that very first Sunday he was with them, and Jerry had explained what it was and why it was important to Christians. The bread (cracker) and the water, which was substituted for grape juice, represented the body and blood of Christ. Jerry had told Ned they always did this to remember the sacrifice of Christ on the cross for the sins of men.

Ned still seemed a little puzzled but said nothing.

Day 50

Jerry was up at his usual time on that Monday morning, drinking his coffee and having his time alone with God. At 0700, everyone else had woken, doing their twenty minutes of exercises. By 0830, Jerry was ready to explore the road to the east. He and Ned dragged the Kawasaki out of the cave, gassed it up from Jerry's five-gallon gas can, and checked the oil. Jerry packed a snack in his backpack, strapped on his Glock and knife. After final instructions to the others on what they should do while he was gone, he kissed April and was off down the hill, where he turned east on the dirt road. Glancing at the sky, he noted it still had that amber tinge, but the color seemed fainter each day.

The road allowed a steady climb for about ten miles, then it ascended more sharply. When Jerry could see the crest of the hill, he stopped the bike and laid it in the grade line. He crept to the top, keeping a low profile, and carefully scanned the valley below him. There was no movement. Then his eyes fell on a small cabin about a mile away and about a hundred yards off the road. He carefully watched for almost ten minutes. No sign of life.

Back on the bike, he slowly made his way down the mountain. When he was opposite the cabin, he rode as close as possible, set the bike aside, and approached the cabin. The windows were boarded up. He tried the door. It was stuck, but with a turn of the knob and a push with his shoulder, it opened.

He could see a door opposite the front door. He opened it to let in more light. It appeared to be a ranger cabin, complete with a sink, old pitcher pump, bunk beds, and a large, freestanding cabinet. Opening the cabinet, he found a magnificent cache. It was fully stocked with canned goods consisting of fruit, vegetables, coffee, and meat. He could hardly believe his eyes. On the bottom shelf were two large five-gallon cans, tightly sealed. One was labeled "flour" and the other "corn meal." What a treasure, he thought. Then he said aloud, "Thank you, Lord, thank you."

Jerry wasted no time. After putting a couple of cans in his backpack, he shut both doors and quickly retreated to the bike. On the road, he drove as fast as safely possible.

Everyone was surprised to see Jerry back so soon, asking him if something was wrong.

"Nothing is wrong! Everything is wonderful! God is good!" Jerry almost shouted the words. He told them what he had found.

It was getting late in the day—too late to make the trek back to the cabin. Jerry decided to ride the dirt bike to the SUV and be ready to leave the original campsite early the next morning. He told Ned to meet him at 0600 hours below the cave.

At 0555 hours, Ned was waiting in the grade line below the cave. Jerry picked him up then continued to drive with the lights off—he could make out the road pretty well. It was daylight by the time they got close to the cabin. Jerry was able to drive to within twenty yards of the cabin.

It took several trips but working as fast as they could, they cleaned out the pantry. They found some old blankets and straw mats on the bunk beds and took those too. The SUV was stuffed full when they finally headed for the cave.

When they arrived, everyone pitched in and carried the canned goods and supplies. By 1300 hours, Jerry was on his way back to the original campsite. He loaded the seats back in the SUV, then disabled and camouflaged it. He was back at the cave by 1500 hours, and he was worn out. Jerry lay down, only intending to take a quick nap, but he didn't wake up until after midnight. He sat up for a moment, then rolled over, kissed his wife, and fell asleep again.

Day 52

After their usual morning routine of exercise and breakfast, they began to organize and inventory their new supplies. Jerry opened the can of flour, hoping it was not wormy. But he said if it were, they would pick the worms out and use the flour anyway, or they could just eat the little critters. "We could use the "extra protein," he said with a grin, while the others made faces and gagging sounds.

Both the flour and meal were okay. The cans had been tightly sealed and the cabin had been cool. They could have bread or cornbread almost every meal if they liked. The twenty pounds of sugar was lumpy and hard but usable.

Ned made a fire, boiled some water, and washed the blankets. He and Thor would sleep comfortably now, even when the temperature dropped.

Day 70

Jerry was taking a nap in the afternoon. The boys and Ned were playing cards. April decided she would take a little walk in the woods. She had not walked very far when she heard some leaves rustling and what sounded like a twig snapping. She stood perfectly still. Looking to her left, she saw a medium-sized buck rubbing his head against a small tree.

She very quietly crouched low and carefully slipped back toward the cave. She reached inside the cave entrance and picked up the .223, which was always fully loaded. No one seemed to notice her—Jerry was still napping, and the boys were arguing over whose turn it was to deal.

April moved quietly back to the area where she had seen the buck. She only moved a foot or so at a time. The buck was rubbing his head and neck against the bark of the tree. He seemed to be enjoying his little massage. He was only about twenty-five yards away. April could not remember ever having a better shot in all the times she had been hunting. She took careful aim. Her hands were as steady as a rock. She took a breath, let half of it out, and squeezed the trigger, just like she had learned in basic training. The bullet struck the deer in the heart, right behind his left front shoulder. He lunged forward about twenty feet and fell. He kicked two or three times and then was still.

April noted exactly where he lay and ran back toward

the cave. She was met halfway by Jerry and the boys. The shot had startled them. Jerry had his Glock unholstered and a wild-eyed look on his face.

April just smiled at him and said, "Bring your hunting knife; we have meat for supper."

Jerry and the boys bled out Mr. Buck and field-dressed him where he lay. They found a tree not far from the cave with a perfect limb for hanging the carcass. They had steaks that night, stew the next day, and they roasted some the day after. Jerry cut the rest of it up into strips and began to smoke them over a low fire in the cave. They found some mountain laurel wood and slivered it off to keep the wood smoldering under the strips of venison. The fire had to be tended every few hours so it didn't go out or get too hot. Within a few days, they had some pretty tasty venison jerky.

TEN

Lone Wolves, Sleeper Cells, and Hoodlums

America was in trouble. The sleeper cells had been joined by malcontent young hoodlums. They were not as interested in destroying what was left of America as they were in simply looting. When these loosely organized sleeper cells discovered that these young people didn't believe the way they believed, they either killed them or drove them off. Martial law did not actually help much because few people knew about it and there were fewer people to enforce it.

The most effective force against these lone wolves and sleeper cells were small militia groups. They were made up of farmers, ranchers, and blue-collar workers who were tired of being pushed around. Well-armed, well-organized, and well-disciplined, these militia members were often members of the NRA and veterans who had served in several wars that America, such as Vietnam, Iraq, and Afghanistan.

When the militia learned of a sleeper cell in the

area, they stalked them and wiped them out with well-coordinate surprise attacks.

ELEVEN

Day 90, Winter in Colorado

The snow had come to northeast Colorado. The Hunt family, which pretty much now included Ned, had made a doorway of sorts at the front of the cave—they'd stacked small logs on top of each other and used their ponchos over the top to cut the wind. The cave was definitely cozy in terms of space, with just a small crawl hole for entering and exiting.

The smoke hole at the back of the cave was checked every evening for clogs—and so far, there were no problems. It was indeed like living within a huge fireplace. Fresh air was drawn into the front entrance, which fed the fire. The carbon monoxide was drawn out of the chimney along with the smoke. The stone walls held the heat, and the temperature stayed at a very comfortable sixty-six to sixty-eight degrees.

Boredom was the enemy now.

Day 180

The routine did not change until one day in March when they saw water coming through the chimney hole. The snow was beginning to melt. Everyone went out and stomped around in the snow. Thor romped around and barked with excitement. The air felt warm. Jerry said they would need to replenish the supplies within another month or so.

A week later, Jerry rode the dirt bike to the old campsite to check on the SUV. It was exactly as he had left it. He hoped the battery was still up. He replaced the fuel pump fuse, held his breath, and turned the key. It turned slowly at first and then it fired up. Jerry knew it needed to run a while to charge the battery. He ran it at a fast idle for thirty minutes. He could not do anything about the tracks in the snow around the SUV, so he just disabled it again and went back to the cave.

Day 190, Early Spring

Jerry had a family meeting. He listened to everyone who had a suggestion. He had already made up his mind what he was going to do. But it was good to allow everyone to put their two cents in.

April said she wanted to get out of the cave next time Jerry went somewhere.

Two days later, Jerry told April he was going to take

a little excursion to find out any updates on what was happening now—and remembering her request, he asked her to join him. After a good night's sleep, Jerry and April were up before daylight. Waking the boys, he gave last-minute instructions and hugs all around. Jerry reminded them that he and April might be gone for as long as three days.

He also reminded April that it would take almost four hours to walk the fifteen miles to the SUV, depending on how much snow was on the road. She still wanted to go. They were in better shape than he'd thought, it turned out—they did it in three hours and fifteen minutes.

Jerry turned north on the hard-surfaced road and drove to the crossroad store/filling station where he had met Frank Shockley. There was a fairly large group of men and a few women hanging around out front. Frank concealed his Glock but kept it on him. He could see that most of the people were also armed. He left April in the Yukon. The old man who had been sitting beside the candy case that first day recognized Jerry and said, "Hey, we haven't seen you for a while." Jerry shook hands with the man and went into the store. Frank Shockley was behind the counter with his magnificent Dirty Harry— the .357 Magnum—on his hip. He also remembered Jerry and started a friendly conversation.

Jerry noticed the shelves were almost empty of goods. He went to the front of the store and motioned for April to join him. He introduced April all around. Jerry told them he had been holed up for the winter, but guessed they could tell that by his beard. They laughed because all the men had beards. Jerry was hungry for news, and so Frank filled him in on what he knew.

Then Frank asked Jerry if he would be interested in joining their militia group. He said they could always use some good people. He first wanted to know some of Jerry's background. He was impressed with both Jerry and April when he learned they were former military. Jerry was careful to not reveal exactly where they were holed up, but if these folks could use the help, Jerry and April were willing to serve.

Frank offered the Hunts some coffee and homemade donuts. At about 1100 hours, a tall, silver-haired man, who walked ramrod straight, came into the store. He was a serious-looking man with a square jaw and cold, blue eyes.

Frank introduced him as Major Charles Stewart, US Army Ret. He shook hands with a very firm grip. It was only after he learned of the Hunts' military background that he smiled broadly.

The major didn't mince words. He offered Jerry and April a place to stay if they wanted to move out of their cave and come join their unit. An old couple who owned a farmhouse about a mile or so down the road had died over the winter and their house was empty. No one had heard from the couple's only child, a daughter who lived in New York City. She was presumed dead, and the major guessed her passing was likely what had caused the deaths of the old couple. Someone said, "They died of a broken heart."

Jerry asked if anyone had heard about rural folks coming down with illnesses related to the attack, such as radiation sickness. The answer was: not yet, but probably in areas closer to the large cities—at least that was the rumor. Jerry supposed it would eventually catch up to them, but so far, so good.

Jerry informed the major that they had three more people back at the cave—two preteen boys and another in his late teens. He suggested the boys would be able to help in some ways as well. This seemed to please the major very much.

After saying their goodbyes, Jerry and April went to check out the farmhouse. They could see right away it would do very nicely. It would be far more comfortable than the cave. They also felt safer among these fine folks at the "Crossroads."

Back at the cave, they had a quick meeting and were all in agreement to move to the farmhouse, acknowledging that it would take a couple of trips to move everything. The cave had served its purpose.

They loaded all the food in the Yukon and started out for the Crossroads. Ned followed on the Kawasaki.

After the second trip, they were all moved in. April said cheerfully, "We have everything we need—table, chairs, beds, and even silverware." The boys piped up, "And a bathroom." The pantry was bare, but other than that, their basic needs were covered, and then some.

There were three bedrooms downstairs and a large room upstairs. April and Jerry took the room next to the bathroom. Ned had a room to himself. Lon and Jon shared a room and a bed for now. Jerry took the upstairs as a study and a lookout point.

The major had told them that the militia met all day every Saturday and every Wednesday night for two hours. This militia unit was known as "Stewart's Rangers." The local volunteer fire department had given each militia family a two-way radio that could now be used in an emergency, as they had a generator which could be fired up. When the major found that Ned had a dirt bike, he asked him if he could serve as a courier to carry messages in a pinch. Ned gladly accepted this responsibility.

Food and gasoline were a large concern for Jerry, and he asked the major and Frank for their thoughts on how they would maintain enough of each. Frank said they were expecting a large truckload of supplies from Canada just as soon as the roads were clear up north. They were also expecting a supply of gasoline from Oklahoma any day. The federal government had recovered enough under the leadership of Paul Ryan to be able to supply the various militia groups with supplies at no cost.

The militias were not just for defense of their communities now. Many of them sought out ISIS groups as well, wiping them out.

TWELVE

A couple of days after the Hunts had moved in, a man came up the lane, leading a cow. Thor alerted them to a stranger in the yard with his persistent barking. The stranger opened the gate and turned the cow into the barnyard.

He came to the door and took off his cap when April opened it. He had a sheepish look on his face. He said, "Madam, my name is Bill Fife. I brought the cow back that belongs here. When the old couple died, I took the cow to my barn and milked her every day. But now that you're here, I figured this is where she should be."

At the sound of the commotion, Jerry came down from his study and introduced himself. When he heard about the cow, he said, "We're much obliged, Bill, but I know nothing about milking a cow. You can take her back home. If you have extra milk, I will buy some from you."

Bill's eyes brightened as he smiled and said, "Why, thank you so much. I tell you what I am going to do; when she throws a calf this summer, I will bring it to you to have for your very own."

The next day a Ford Ranger pickup pulled in the drive. Sipping on his second cup of coffee, Jerry eyeballed him from the kitchen as an elderly man got out and knocked on the door, which Jerry promptly opened.

The man was about seventy years old with a twinkle in his eye and a sly smile on his face. He held out his hand in greeting. "Mr. Hunt, my name is James Jordan," he said. Jerry shook his hand and nodded for him to continue. "I live a couple of miles up the road, and . . . well, I've brought you some chickens. Belonged to the folks who used to live here, but when they died, I collected their chickens and put them up with mine. Seein' as you're here now, I am bringing them back because . . . well, because they're not mine."

Jerry grinned, thinking of Bill Fife with the cow. "That's okay, James. Go ahead and keep them. You've made sure they stayed alive and well."

James shook his head. "No sir, I get enough eggs from mine, and I'm sure with these young'uns around here, you can use the eggs."

Jerry could see that the old man wouldn't take no for an answer, and they definitely could use the eggs. So they uncrated the dozen chickens, ten of which were hens, into the chicken yard.

"What do you feed them anyway?" Jerry asked, scratching his head as he watched the birds scooting about.

"I have some corn and oats in the truck, but if you run out and can't get more, just feed 'em table scraps."

The hens must have recognized the place because they went straight into the chicken house. However, they didn't start laying again for three or four days. The eggs were a huge treat for the family—it had been six months since any of them had eaten an egg.

One Friday late in the afternoon, an emergency meeting of Stewart's Rangers was called. They met at the station for the Crossroads Volunteer Fire Department. There were thirty-eight men and women in all.

Some strange men in strange vehicles had been seen near the Crossroads. Everyone needed to be extra vigilant. They would start a patrol that evening until the people left the area or until they were arrested, if they were found to be dangerous.

That night a patrol of four men in a king-cab pickup made the rounds. Jerry was among those men. He was armed with his Glock and an AR-15 that Major Stewart had supplied him. Off in a wooded area, they saw a small bonfire. They turned off the lights and approached the fire quietly on foot from two sides. They moved close enough to hear men talking low. It was a foreign language—not Spanish . . . maybe Arabic.

They counted eight men, but there could have been more in any of the three vehicles parked near the fire. The leader of the militia that night was Lt. Douglas Phillips.

He signaled for the group to retreat to the truck. Lieutenant Phillips said they would alert more men, then converge and overwhelm the intruders. They made rounds to most of the homes of the militia and gathered a force. Major Stewart would lead.

They figured the best time to attack would be around 0400 hours. Their plan was to sneak up on them like last time, secure the vehicles, and approach the group on the ground from two sides. They would throw a flash bomb into the midst of them. If any reached for weapons, they were to be shot immediately.

Twenty men approached the area at 0345 hours. Six militiamen stood at the three vehicles. At precisely 0400 hours, a flash bomb was thrown. The loud bang, flash, and smoke brought ten of the enemy to their feet. Lieutenant Phillips shouted, "Freeze, and put up your hands!"

They must have understood because immediately hands went up, and no one moved. Two of the militia moved through the enemy and secured weapons. They carefully searched each one and found explosives as well as many handguns and automatic rifles. There was also a

Korean-style bazooka with three rounds. They were not squirrel hunting; that was for sure.

Only two of them admitted to speaking English. One of the militiamen questioned the two who spoke English while Major Stewart stood by. After the men were questioned for about half an hour, Major Stewart turned away, a disgusted expression on his face. He said to no one in particular, "We should have shot the bastards! They're not going to tell us anything. Besides that, what are we going to do with them?"

They were handcuffed with thick plastic tie wraps. Major Stewart contacted the state police, who radioed the National Guard. By 1200 hours, a National Guard personnel carrier with eight men arrived at the Crossroads and took the prisoners into custody.

Stewart's Rangers kept two of the three enemy vehicles—a Ford F-150 and a Chevy Silverado. The Guardsmen took the prisoners away in the personnel carrier and the third truck, a Toyota Tundra.

Stewart's Rangers now had two more pickup trucks, several more AR-15s, and several thousand rounds of ammunition—the spoils of war. The National Guard took the bazooka and the three rounds that went with it.

At the Saturday meeting, Major Stewart debriefed the unit, commending them on a job well done, but reminding them not to let down their defenses. There was much work to still do. Sleeper cells were increasingly being put out of commission by the military and by little groups like Stewart's Rangers.

⁂

Jerry and April were growing attached to this tight group of people and the whole community. However, now that they were no longer in as much danger, they were feeling very sad about family members who they were sure were dead. The grieving set in when they had time to think about these things.

April found Ned on the front porch one morning, crying as if his heart were broken. She put her arms around him and hugged him tight. After he stopped sobbing, he said, "I'm sorry, but I have no other family. I'm an only child, and my grandparents died when I was small. I'm all alone. What am I going to do?"

April didn't know what to say, so she just put her arm around his shoulder and said a prayer for him.

Later, April discussed the situation with Jerry, who said, "You know, we could adopt Ned. But regardless, he can stay with us for the rest of his life, if he wants."

Relieved, April wholeheartedly agreed. The Hunts had become quite fond of Ned.

THIRTEEN

The Stranger

Almost a year to the day from when Ned saw the flash and was knocked off his dirt bike, he and Jerry were at Frank's place, down at the Crossroads.

A ragged figure pushing a bicycle loaded down with a blanket, clothes, and a backpack slung over the handlebars came up the road. From a distance, they couldn't tell if it was a man or a woman. Nor could one tell the age. The figure walked like an old person, with an unsteady rocking motion. He/she collapsed on the old bench out front. The stranger took off a filthy baseball cap and shook out long hair. Lo and behold, it was a girl! She looked to be maybe fifteen years old, at the most.

Jerry approached her, and she cringed as if he were going to hit her. He spoke softly, trying to reassure her. "Don't be afraid; we won't hurt you." He told Ned to go and get April, and to "hurry." Ned spun the tires as he drove off in the Yukon.

Frank Shockley came out of the building with a bottle

of water in hand, which he gave to Jerry, who gave it to the girl. She struggled with the bottle cap, so Jerry took it back, opened it, and handed it to her. She guzzled it all down within a couple of minutes. Jerry asked her when she had eaten last. She didn't answer, but she shook her head and shrugged her shoulders. Finally, she said, "My name is Rachael Byrd." Then she just slumped, unconscious, on the bench. Jerry shifted her so she was lying across the bench.

April and Ned roared up, in short order. April's confused expression turned to one of concern when Jerry told her that young Rachael appeared to be a mighty sick girl. They loaded her into the Yukon and took her to the house, where they took her to Ned's room and laid her on the bed. She could not have weighed more than eighty-five pounds. She felt like skin and bones.

⸻

April ran everyone out of the room, locked the door, and began to undress her. As she pulled the clothing off her, it became obvious she was probably older than fifteen—more like twenty. As April struggled to get her out of the nasty clothes, Rachael began to fight her. "No, no, don't do that," she whimpered. April soothed her, telling her it was all right, that she was safe. Finally, the girl got very quiet. April tiptoed out of the room and told the fellows to stay away from the girl.

She told Jerry, "I think this girl has been abused badly. I am going to sleep in her room tonight."

That night, April stayed close to Rachael, soothing her with kind words and gently rubbing her back. Her heart went out to the girl, as did her prayers.

Jerry arose early, as was his custom. The aroma of coffee brought April awake earlier than her usual. She sat and drank a cup with Jerry as he quietly read his Bible. After about ten minutes, he reached over and took April's hand, bowed his head, and prayed. He thanked God that they had been able to help this girl named Rachael Byrd. He thanked the Lord for his wife and family. And he thanked the Lord for leading them to this place. Jerry asked God for wisdom, courage, and for the salvation of America. He so wanted America to be as it had been when he was a boy, but suspected those days were gone for good. At the end of his prayer, he simply said, "I praise your holy name, and please give us a good day. In His name I pray. Amen."

When Ned came down from upstairs where he had slept in a sleeping bag, he asked about "the girl," and April told him that she had slept fairly well all night. A couple hours later, April checked on Rachael, quietly entering the room. The girl rolled over and then sat bolt upright, a wild look in her eyes. April smiled at her and sat on the bed.

"Would you like some breakfast?"

Rachael cleared her throat and squeaked out, "Yes mum."

April stuck her head out of the door and asked Jerry to start some breakfast. She then found a robe to wrap her in and went into the bathroom and poured several cans of water in the tub. After heating several more pans of water on the gas stove, April warmed the water in the tub and led Rachael to the bathroom. She laid out towels, washrags, and soap for her, and told her to put on the robe when she was through.

After a wonderful breakfast of scrambled eggs, grits, toast, and coffee, Rachael looked much better. She had beautiful auburn hair and was a very pretty young lady. She volunteered that she was from the Denver area. She had been on the road, sleeping in barns and fields for months. A group of men had come upon her in a barn where she was sleeping and had made her stay with them for several weeks. They had forced themselves upon her and had beaten her. She said she didn't think they were Arabic, but just a gang of men taking advantage of a lawless society. She had finally gotten away from them late one night after they had looted a liquor store and were in a drunken stupor.

She was nineteen years old and had been in college when the bombing took place. She had no idea what had happened to her family. Her dad was a doctor, and her mother was a teacher. She had a fifteen-year-old brother.

As she spoke about her family, her whole body began to shake as she sobbed. April wrapped her arms around her, soothed her, and kissed her on the forehead. They'd all lost something in this mess. How much more could they lose?

Rachael's clothes were in such bad shape that April just threw them in the trash. She wrapped Rachael up in a clean, warm blanket and told her she would be back in a little bit.

April drove down to the Crossroads and asked Thelma Shockley if she knew where they could find some very petite clothes for Rachael. Thelma said she thought she could scrounge up some things. She would bring them to the house.

When April got back home, Rachael was surrounded by Jerry and the boys, and seemed more at ease. She was the star of the show. Lon and Jon were talking up a storm to her and asking all kinds of questions.

Finally, April said, "Okay guys, back off." The boys scurried outside, but Ned and Jerry stuck around to help make room for Rachael. Ned would move upstairs, and they would need to find additional bedding for him, maybe some bunkbeds for the boys too.

The Hunts had already decided that she would stay with them.

Thelma showed up with a box and a plastic bag full of clothes. All that afternoon, Rachael tried on clothes. To her delight, she discovered there were several pairs of jeans and blouses that fit her well. Jon had a pair of tennis shoes that would fit her if she wore extra-thick socks. They were not pretty, but they would do.

When Rachael came to the supper table that evening, the boys and Ned all whistled at her.

She blushed. "Stop it, just stop it." But her grin said she was happy with the compliments.

Third Sunday in August

Every Sunday morning Jerry called the family to worship at 0900 hours.

He had asked Frank, Thelma, Doug Phillips, Major Stewart, and their families if they would like to worship with them. So far, they had declined the offer.

The worship began with an opening prayer by one of the boys. April started a song and all joined in. Jerry opened his Bible and "brought a lesson," as he called it, from the New Testament.

Ned still thought Jerry could preach better and more understandably than any ordained preacher he had ever heard—of course, he had not heard many.

There was always a prayer time in which anyone could pray if they wanted. April and the boys always prayed.

Then Jerry would close. But this Sunday at prayer time, Ned said he would like to pray. He prayed a very short but powerful prayer, asking God to bless the Hunts and their new friend Rachael. Finally, it was time for communion.

The Hunts were now using a grape drink since the new supplies had come. April had baked some piecrust for the bread.

Rachael spoke up and said, "I am a Christian; can I please join you?"

Jerry was embarrassed that he had failed to ask her. "Sure, sweetheart, this is not my supper; it is the Lord's."

The service that day was an enriching one as their little "family" grew in the Lord.

FOURTEEN

Year Two

It was the beginning of the second year after the attack on America. Time had been marked from that fateful day in August. No one celebrated the day, but no one forgot it either.

On the 23rd of August, a rural electric power truck drove to the Crossroads and told Frank Shockley to pass the word that the power would be coming back on that afternoon at three o'clock. Word spread quickly. Most people made sure that the switches were off to the main breaker boxes. No one wanted to be accidentally electrocuted.

At 1505 hours, Jerry began to slowly flip the breakers in the house. They had lights in all the rooms. He told everyone to keep a sharp eye out for smoke, sparks, or signs of anything burning. The refrigerator was plugged in. The light came on, but it would likely be hours before they would know if it would keep things cold. The clothes dryer and washer worked. The big chest freezer on the back porch buzzed and kicked the breaker off. It was likely shot. Jon turned the TV on, but the screen was blank. The radio that Jerry and April had in the bedroom came on, but they could only find one station—music with about five minutes of news every fifteen minutes. But there was no news they didn't already know. It was the same station they could get on the radio in the Yukon.

The water they had used up to that point came from a water wagon the National Guard had brought to the Crossroads for the community to use. They carried several five-gallon cans of water home in the Yukon every day.

Now with some electricity, things were looking up in terms of water—Jerry found the water pump in the well house was running, although it needed to be primed since it had been off so long. After about fifteen minutes, water was running in the house, and the hot water heater was working. There would be baths all around that night.

Jerry called a family meeting just before supper that evening. After everyone had gathered round the table, Jerry opened his Bible and read one of David's praises from the book of Psalms. Then everyone joined hands for prayer. April began, and each one said a prayer after her; some were short and shallow, while others were more mature prayers. All were grateful ones.

Only a few power grids had come back on, and some didn't stay on for very long periods of time. Once a day at 1800 hours, a TV newscast came on that lasted an hour—instead of commercials, there were public service announcements. America was slowly getting to her feet.

Hundreds of thousands of people had died instantly on that fateful day. And people were still dying daily of radiation sickness. Other lung and pulmonary diseases debilitated thousands more. In many cities, people had been buried in mass graves and covered with lime to keep disease at a minimum.

Every day Jerry thanked God that he and his family had been in the rural areas when it all started. He also asked God to send a miracle and bring Rachael's and Ned's families back to them.

The propane tank that had been heating the house was just about empty. Jerry knew they would have to find a different way to heat the house. He was pleased to find a large cast-iron wood heater in the barn. After he and the boys lugged the wood heater into the living room, they hooked up the stovepipe that ran to the chimney. Before they tried it out, Jerry went up on the roof and dropped down a large brick on a rope. He dragged it up and down several times to clean out the creosote. When he was satisfied it was safe, they fired it up with some wood that was still in a woodpile. The wood heater worked like a charm. Now they would need to cut and split some wood.

About fifteen men and boys all got together one

Saturday. They found a nice stand of medium-sized hardwoods that belonged to a farmer, who gave them permission to cut as many trees as they needed, with just one stipulation—they had to cut and split enough wood for him for the winter.

Many hands made light work. Two Saturdays straight they felled trees. They waited a couple of weeks and when the sign of the moon was right, they began to cut and split that wood. For you see, the wood needed to be cut in the right sign or it wouldn't burn right. At least that was what the old-timers said.

The old-timers taught Jerry something else too. It was just like they said: "Wood heats two times. You are warmed when you cut and split it, and warmed again when you burn it."

One September morning, Rachael came out of her room looking pale and with a distressed expression on her face. She asked April if she could talk to her alone. They went back into her room and sat on the bed. Rachael wept softly as she said, "I think I am pregnant." She had not had her period in two months, and she was feeling sick to her stomach every morning.

April held her tightly and said, "It's all right; we will still take care of you, but we need to see if we can find a doctor."

April spoke with Thelma Shockley about a doctor. There was supposed to be an old retired doctor about thirty miles away in a village called Silver Lode. Fortunately, up to this point no one had needed a doctor. Thelma was curious, but April said she couldn't tell her anything further right now.

The next morning after getting directions, Jerry and April took Rachael to Silver Lode, Colorado—just a spot in the road with only four houses and a small weather-beaten store. At the store, they were told the doctor, whom they called "Doc Tom," was in the last house on the end. At the house, a bent-over, old lady answered Jerry's knock at the door. April asked if the doctor was in.

"I reckon I am," the little lady replied with a smile.

April and Jerry looked at each other, surprised.

"I suppose you expected someone younger, or a man perhaps?"

April said, "Well, yes, with a name like Tom . . ."

Doc Tom laughed and said, "Well, my daddy wanted a boy, but actually my last name is Thompson, so I just became Doc Tom when I graduated from the university. Come on in and tell me what I can do for you."

April spoke while Jerry held Rachael's trembling hand. She told how Rachael had been raped repeatedly by thugs. Doc Tom asked some questions and said she needed to run some blood tests to make sure she didn't have an STD of any kind. She had a small laboratory in the back of her house, along with a spotless exam room. Jerry excused himself back to the SUV and let the ladies talk among themselves.

After the exam, it was confirmed that Rachael was indeed several weeks pregnant. The doctor asked her what she wanted to do about it.

"Well, I don't believe in abortions. If I can, I'll carry this baby to term and keep it," Racheal said.

April squeezed her hand and said she agreed with the decision; she and the family would assist any way she could.

The good doctor gave Rachael some calcium and iron pills she had on hand. She told her to eat well and exercise, and to come back and see her in a month.

"What about payment?" April asked. "We have some cash, but my husband is also an electrician, plumber, and a pretty fair mechanic if you need any of those services."

Doc Tom said "For now I am fine. I'll keep him in mind."

The winter was a rough one that year. Dirty snow fell from what could now be described as just a light-amber sky, and the temperature often bottomed at twenty below zero. They kept a heat bulb burning in the well house so the water wouldn't freeze. The Red Cross and Salvation Army had sent surplus army blankets—two blankets per person. No one could pay the electric bill, but the current was never cut off. The government was still providing assistance.

Jerry was not too keen on this—he had never taken a handout before. But he swallowed his pride and just said, "Thank you, Lord, for your provision."

When spring came, Jerry vowed to put his mechanical skills to work. The weather had warmed up enough to be able to spend time outside, so he began to tinker with an old 135 Massey Ferguson tractor in the barn. It didn't look like it had been started in quite a while. The battery was dead and likely shot. After checking the oil and coolant, Jerry drained the gas tank and the carburetor. The gas had gone bad and turned to varnish. He flushed the tank and took the carburetor apart so he could clean the pieces. He removed the spark plugs, cleaned, and gapped them. After putting everything back together, he put a couple of precious gallons of gas in the tank.

He connected the jumper cables from the Yukon to the tractor, flipped the ignition switch, and hit the starter button. It slowly cranked, fired, and died. He waited a few minutes, pulled the choke, and turned the key again. This time it fired and started with a big puff of smoke out of the stack. Now this was a three-cylinder Perkins engine—both powerful and economical to run. And this one sounded like new. Jerry shut it off. When the ground warmed up, he would plow a garden for his family.

All the while, Ned, Lon, and Jon participated with great interest in the mechanics of the tractor. They handed Jerry tools, asked questions . . . and Jerry schooled them in Engine Mechanics 101.

They all cheered when the old Massey Ferguson had fired up and stayed running. Jerry took a deep bow and acted like he did this every day.

At the supper table that night, the boys and Ned all bragged about what a great mechanic Jerry was. He let them brag, but he knew the Lord had given him that skill and knowledge. When he prayed for the meal and the blessings of the day, he gave God the glory. Everyone said, "Amen."

Jerry had put the word out that he was looking for some bunk beds. None could be found; however, one of the men in the militia was a cabinetmaker by trade. He drove up in his old Chevy pickup one day with a set of bunk beds that he had made out of shipping pallets. They were beautiful. Jerry asked what he wanted for them. But the man said, "Tell you what, next time I need an electrician, plumber, or mechanic, you can do the work, and we'll call it even."

They still needed some mattresses. The next day a lady came by who said she had a queen-size mattress stored in her attic. He could have it if he could haul it. However, she had a short in a lamp that needed to be fixed, and she wondered if she could trade out the mattress for the work on the lamp.

And so, a new system of barter and trade came about in the Crossroads community.

Jerry and Ned tied the mattress to the top of the Yukon and brought it home. They cut the mattress lengthwise with a hunting knife and a pair of shears he had found in the barn. April patched the cut sides to keep the stuffing inside. These mattresses fit perfectly on the bunk beds. Now everyone had a comfortable bed to sleep on.

FIFTEEN

The New Arrival
On a Fine Spring Day in April

The labor pains started at five in the morning. Jerry brought Thelma to the house to assist April with the birth of Racheal's baby. By noon, the pains were close and intense, and the labor and delivery unfolded thankfully without problems. Jerry noted in his journal the time of birth at 1425 hours. A beautiful baby girl. Using an old bathroom scale, she weighed in at roughly five and a half pounds. Rachael named her Faith. Faith Byrd.

When the ladies of the community heard the good news, they brought gifts of homemade blankets and all sorts of knitted things for the baby. One of the women had cut up a flannel bed sheet and sewn diapers for little Faith. Bill Fife, the man with the cow, brought fresh milk every other day and would not take a penny for it.

The baby's first name was Faith and perhaps her middle name should have been Hope, for she had restored hope to the small town. She was the first baby born in the Crossroads community since the attack the year before.

Way back in March, an old hermit of a man who lived several miles away had posted a public service announcement on the bulletin board at Frank Shockley's store. He had some garden seed that he was giving away, as long as it lasted—this seed came from all his vegetables from three years before. Jerry wasted no time in contacting the man and picking up some seed. The man made Jerry promise that if he got a crop, he would save some seed and pass some on to others. Jerry gladly made that promise.

Admittedly, Jerry didn't know much about gardening. But when he got the two-bottom plow hooked up, several people stopped by and gave him some pointers. They also asked if he would plow a garden spot for them. Most of the farmers in the area were focusing on plowing and planting their large fields, and not able to make time to plow small gardens. So Jerry put the old tractor, plow, and disc to work. He traded his efforts for things he and his family needed.

One man filled his gas tank from his overhead tank. A woman gave him twenty pounds of last year's potatoes, which he used mainly for seed potatoes. Another family gave him some clothes that fit the boys. Then there was oil and antifreeze for the tractor. Another man gave him a salvaged battery out of a junked truck, which fit the Massey Ferguson perfectly.

A local beautician offered to fix April's hair and even offered to give her a perm if she so desired. April was excited about this, because she had not done anything with her hair for almost two years, except to wash it and trim the ends once in a while.

One older lady had a small chest freezer. It still ran, but she didn't use it. Jerry said he would gladly take it in trade.

After the vegetable garden was plowed, disked, and planted, everyone had to weed and cultivate it. Every morning, instead of exercises, there was hoeing, pulling, and picking peas, butterbeans, string beans, okra, peppers, and tomatoes. The land was rich; they had also used chicken manure between the rows. Most of the seed came up, and by midsummer, they were getting fresh vegetables. They found canning jars and supplies in the fruit cellar under the back porch. With the canning jars and the new freezer, they should be set for next winter. Jerry carefully saved all the seed he could from the vegetables.

He had also plowed and disked an acre behind the barn in order to plant field corn. He bought twenty-five pounds of seed corn from one of the farmers. He had no planter, so he and the family dropped the seeds by hand. He planned to expand his flock of chickens—he wanted to feed them corn in order to have good meat and egg chickens.

Four of his hens had begun to sit on their nests. So he saved some of the eggs and made sure each hen had seven or eight eggs to sit on and hatch. By the end of June, there were twenty chicks following these hens around in the garden, scratching and eating the bugs. It was a great way to fatten the chickens and get rid of pests at the same time.

One day in July, Bill Fife visited the "Hunt house," as it was now called, with a surprise. When April opened the door, there stood this smiling man and, behind him, a beautiful red calf with a white face. He had a rope around its neck, but it was tame as a kitten, gently butting him in the back of his legs. The boys came out and began to pet it.

"Is it a boy or a girl?" Jon asked as he looked under the belly of the cow.

It's a heifer," Bill said.

They were now in the cattle business . . . like it or not.

***

Without a lot of technology, time often seemed to stand still. In many ways, it was like life had been in the early 1900s. Perhaps it was God's way of slowing people down. Light industries opened up. The cabinetmaker became a building contractor. Jerry opened an electrical and plumbing business out in the barn. He made a trip to

Canada where he had been able to secure some electrical equipment on consignment.

When he and the building contractor began to do contract work, there were no regulations to follow. They just relied on common sense when it came to building and repairing things. It had been a long time since common sense had been in style.

Three more TV stations came on. They now showed old movies and some old sitcoms from the sixties and seventies. Neighbors watched out for and helped those in greater need than themselves.

Disasters brought out both the worst and the best in people.

Representatives from each of the one hundred counties were chosen to become state legislators. The "Shockley Crossroads" community, as it was now called, selected Frank Shockley to represent the county. Senators from the north and south districts in Colorado were selected to be state senators. Major Charles Stewart was chosen from the northern part of Colorado. The people in Shockley Crossroads begged the two men to not overregulate with unjust laws.

Shockley and Stewart made a solemn promise that they would do their best to be fair and honest and to not tie the hands of the people.

Special elections like this were taking place all over America. People wanted some government, but they did not desire big government. Big government was clumsy and often became corrupt with power. Big government had failed the people. America would come back better, stronger, and with more freedom than ever. She had learned a great lesson.

September

A gang of twelve thugs came thundering into Shockley Crossroads in four exceedingly loud pickups. They went into the store and roughed up Thelma, robbed her of what little cash she had, and took most of the stock on the shelves. They were bold to try this in broad daylight, but they were not too smart.

The militiamen's radios went off as Thelma placed an alarm out on hers. Within fifteen minutes, almost forty men and women armed to the teeth converged on the store. The thugs had no idea what a hornets' nest they had stepped in. Four loads of militia arrived from two directions at one time. Eight more screeched to a stop within another sixty seconds.

Lt. Doug Philips had a bullhorn and ordered the men to immediately throw down their weapons or they would be shot on the spot.

Now when the first four truckloads of militia came up, the thugs had just laughed at them. But when all forty members of Stewart's Rangers pulled down on them, they threw their arms on the ground . . . all except for one loudmouth who was either flat crazy or high on something. He pulled a sawed-off twelve-gauge from under his long trench coat, and cursing them, aimed the gun.

Big mistake. At least thirty shots rang out almost simultaneously. He was dead before he hit the ground. The rest of the gang seemed in shock as they were rounded up. They were thoroughly searched, and their hands were tied behind their backs.

When Sheriff McNeal arrived, he confiscated all their property and prepared to take them to the next county where there was a jail. Before he left, McNeal asked a few questions about the dead man. Forty people confessed it was self-defense, and that concluded the investigation. Outlaws would not be tolerated. Justice would be swift. The surviving outlaws would be tried by a panel of five Superior Court judges from different parts of the state at some point in the next ninety days.

SIXTEEN

Yes, the wool had been pulled over the eyes of the American government. However, when ISIS tried to finish the destruction they had started, they found they were not dealing with France or Germany. Americans had weapons, and they had the will to survive and fight back. The terrorist's attacks became fewer as the militia groups and individuals fought fiercely against them.

America's population had been reduced almost overnight by more than fifty percent. There were now less than 150 million people. Many of these would likely die within five years.

Some cities, such as New York, Chicago, and Los Angeles, would not be inhabitable for perhaps a hundred years. However, many of the other large cities had only been hit by low levels of radiation and would once again be livable in a dozen years or so.

The Great Plains, desert areas, and mountainous areas were becoming more populated as survivors began to migrate. Americans had always been creative when they needed to be. The old saying that "cream rises to the top" was true. There was no doubt a new age of Thomas

Edisons, Henry Fords, and Founding Fathers were born from necessity.

New and more energy-efficient windmills, energy from the sun, and even the old standby oil and gas were now coming on line as sources of energy.

The economy was coming back. The stock exchange was relocated to Indianapolis, which had only been struck by one small, low-yield atom bomb that missed the center of the city. Indianapolis was close to the center of the country, and so it was a strategic place for a new "Wall Street."

On the other hand, banking and investing were slow to return. People who had cash on hand or hidden someplace kept it where it was. The government was thinking of going to a gold-and-silver standard. If they did, then people would likely turn in their cash for new currency that would be guaranteed with gold or silver. Then, and only then, would banks be trusted again.

The new capital of the nation would be near Little Rock, Arkansas, which had amazingly been spared, except for some suitcase and car bombs. Minor changes to the Constitution would make the government work better than ever.

Freedom of speech, religion, and the right to bear arms were strengthened for the citizens of America. All of these things were voted on by representatives from each state, but would at a later date need to be ratified by at least two-thirds of the states.

It was amazing how the people were now pulling together instead of being at odds with each other. Since so many records had been destroyed, all adults were asked to pledge loyalty to America, whether or not they had been citizens at the time of the attack, in order to be considered citizens in the current day.

The military guarded America's borders to the south and to the north. No one except those proving they were citizens of America could enter the country.

In the Great Plains, a new land rush was being planned. Many areas that had been owned by the federal government would be opened up and distributed to the people by drawing lots. Land and property where no one claimed ownership, such as the house where the Hunts now lived, could be claimed by "squatters' rights." However, this was adjudicated by the local county government. In most cases, one had to improve the property within a five-year period.

Schoolhouses that remained intact were once again being used for teaching. In some areas, small community schools sprang up in firehouses, churches, and community buildings with teachers being drawn from other industries. Ministers became school principals. People with four-year degrees in almost any field became teachers where needed. Agriculture, mechanics, electronics, and basic mathematics were required courses for all middle school children and older.

The federal government under the leadership of the new president and new Congress had taken bold steps and abolished the IRS. The tax system was now a consumer tax. Whoever bought anything paid a small tax on it. There were no loopholes for the rich. This tax went directly into the treasury. The tax lawyers howled like scalded dogs, but this was a new day and a new system. It would be difficult to corrupt.

Other large, bulky, and corrupt agencies were under scrutiny and would more than likely be abolished, such as the Environmental Protection Agency and the Department of Education. The Veterans Administration was to be completely overhauled as well. The United Nations, of course, had been destroyed and would never get back on American soil. The country would arise from the ashes on her own, stronger and more determined than ever.

The local militia known as Stewart's Rangers was not disbanded but now held meetings only once a month. Every household became its own security.

The Missing Piece

There seemed to be only one piece of society that had

not immediately started a comeback—the most important piece. Organized religion seemed to be lacking.

Morality was at a higher standard, but formal worship had taken a nosedive. The nearest church building in the Crossroads community was about five miles away; it was a Baptist church with a small congregation of elderly people. Jerry inquired about who owned the building. An old deacon by the name of John Wallace said the Baptist Association owned it, but he had not heard from anybody in that organization in a long time. Jerry asked if he could hold services in the building, and the deacon said he didn't see any reason why not. Of course, they had no preacher.

Jerry explained his plans in more detail. "I want to have a New Testament Church, with strictly New Testament practices, just like the first church at Jerusalem. I want us to call ourselves simply Christians, like the people in Antioch in Acts 11. My family and I always have the Lord's Supper every Lord's Day, and I want to offer it to any Christian who attends."

The old deacon thought a minute and then finally said, "Well, that sounds like a good idea to me." Now, John Wallace was a dyed-in-the-wool Baptist, and he struggled with not having the Baptist name on the church but understood where Jerry was coming from. There was nothing divisive about the words "Christ" or "Christian." Even the Methodists and Presbyterians were not against the words. The idea would work for everyone.

That first Sunday, twelve people were present, counting Jerry and his family. He preached just like the building was full. The next Sunday, there were twenty-eight people present. Word had gotten around about the services. Almost everyone liked the simplicity of it. One older lady wept all through the communion service. She told Jerry later that she had missed communion so very much. She thanked him and hugged his neck.

One Sunday morning at the invitation time, the congregation was singing "Just as I Am." Ned Carney walked forward. He told Jerry he wanted Jesus as his savior. Jerry took his confession of faith. "I believe that Jesus is the Christ, the Son of the living God." Just as they were about to have the closing prayer, two more people came forward—Lon and Jon Hunt.

Jerry looked at April, her eyes welling with tears. The family circle was complete.

Jerry asked Deacon Wallace where they normally baptized people. He said it had been so long he had almost forgotten. But then he recalled, if it were warm enough, they baptized in a little creek a couple of miles away.

It was the fall of the year, but not too chilly just yet. That afternoon, about thirty people met at the small bridge over Raccoon Creek where Ned, Lon, and Jon were immersed for the remission of their sins. The old deacon read some scripture and had a very long, sanctimonious prayer before the baptism.

Jerry had an idea about a baptistery for when the weather got cold. He didn't mention it to anyone else. In his barn was a fair-sized stock watering tank. He tested it to make sure it didn't leak. He asked Frank Shockley if he could borrow his pickup truck because he wanted to move that tank into the church building.

When Frank found out what he wanted to do, he said, "I'll help you." He really wanted to see the look on old Deacon Wallace's face when he found out there was a stock watering tank in the church building.

After it was moved in, Jerry asked the cabinetmaker if he could build a wooden cabinet around the tank so it didn't look like the stock tank that it was. He said he reckoned he could, but he sure wanted to see the look on John Wallace's face before he did.

"No," Jerry said, "I want it built before next Sunday."

The stock tank was set in place next to the stage. A hose could be run through the window to fill it and a portable tank heater placed in it to heat the water. It could be drained in the same way, with a siphon hose. When the cabinetmaker got finished, it looked like a commercial baptistery—at least until one looked down into it. Weather would be no problem now.

All over the country, families that had been separated by the sudden attack were slowly being reunited. Jerry and his family kept praying for Ned and Rachael to be reunited with their families. But as the days went by, the chances grew more remote.

Baby Faith was growing steadily and had become the center of attention of everyone in the community. She was a beautiful baby with dark hair, dark eyes, and long, dark eyelashes. Her complexion was a beautiful, light tan.

SEVENTEEN

Heading East

The garden had produced abundantly. The vegetables were all canned and frozen. Now Jerry wanted to take Ned and head back toward St. Louis to Ned's old home. The young man had seemed a little down lately, and was often seen staring down the road in the direction from which he had come. After considerable discussion, April agreed that perhaps that was what he needed for closure.

Jerry chose some supplies to last about a week and loaded the Yukon. They set out the next morning at 0600 hours with two extra five-gallon cans of gasoline and two sleeping bags.

Jerry used the Road Atlas to find the road Ned had come in on, along with Ned's advice. Things had changed somewhat in two years, but Ned did a good job of directing Jerry. They finally got to a four-lane highway, which Jerry figured should lead to St. Louis. There was precious little traffic to contend with, and so for several hours he put the speedometer on eighty miles per hour. About twenty miles outside of St. Louis, the houses appeared empty. Five more miles and Ned told Jerry to slow down, get off the four-lane, and pull onto a secondary road. He directed Jerry to make a series of turns. Ned suddenly shouted, "There it is! That's my house."

Jerry parked in the driveway and shut off the engine. The front door was open, and they approached the house cautiously. Inside, it appeared the house had been ransacked and looted. There was not much of anything left.

Ned went through the closets and found a man's dress hat on a top shelf, way in the back. He dusted it off, then hugged it to his chest and put it to his nose. Finally placing it on his head, he explained it was his dad's good hat that he only wore on special occasions.

Jerry hugged his shoulder and said, "Looks pretty sharp on you, kid."

They searched some more, and Ned found a silk scarf crumpled up in a corner. Just like he had done with that hat, Ned put it to his nose and sniffed. He looked up at Jerry and said, "It smells like my mom."

However, there was no sign that his folks had ever been back.

They entered the kitchen, and Jerry spied a picture frame under a crumpled newspaper in the kitchen. He turned the frame over, and through a cracked glass, smiling back at him was a man, woman, and a teenager.

The Carney family. He turned and handed the broken picture to Ned, whose tears were already running down his cheeks. Jerry embraced him and said a silent prayer, asking for comfort, strength, and courage for the young man. Jerry could only imagine the heartache.

After Jerry gave Ned some time to wander around the house and the yard, they backed out of the drive and headed toward St. Louis. However, just two miles down the road was a barricade with warning signs to proceed no farther due to radiation. They turned the car around and headed back toward the Crossroads.

Along the way, they found a narrow path where they parked and ate some sandwiches and a can of baked beans. They decided to spend the night as well.

The next morning they got back on a state highway and drove all the way across Kansas at a slower pace than they had come. In the little towns, they could tell they were looked on with suspicion, which was understandable. They looked at strangers who passed through the Crossroads the same way.

When they arrived back at the farmhouse, everyone was eager to hear about their trip. Ned showed them his hat and the scarf. And then he proudly showed them the picture. These artifacts were all he had to remember his folks.

Rachael was desirous to learn more about her folks too, but it would have to be put off for a while until the baby got older and she got stronger. Jerry told her maybe next year, because the snow would soon be flying.

The family was much more prepared for winter than they had been the last two years. But they prayed it would be a mild one so they would not have to thaw pipes and fight the bitter cold.

As it turned out, they were not so fortunate.

It began to snow the last week in October, and they never saw the ground until the last of March. However, the snow was much whiter than the winter before. The temperature dropped to twenty-five below zero several nights, and the highs never got above freezing for a month.

The snow was a blessing, though, as it served as insulation so the below-ground pipes didn't freeze. They kept a roaring fire going in the big old wood heater, where they also cooked and kept coffee at the ready.

Jerry kept the Yukon ready to roll by keeping a couple of two-hundred-watt light bulbs burning under the hood next to the battery and the engine. He cranked it every couple of days and drove to the Crossroads or to the church building. While he was out, he always checked on the older neighbors.

They missed several Sundays going to church due to the severe weather, but they still had services there in the house.

People in the community had started to call Jerry "Preacher." He kind of liked that. He laughed and said, "I have been called a lot worse." But at the same time Jerry was disappointed that few people took worshipping God seriously. Did they not realize that they had been spared while millions had died?

Jerry thought there was not much worse than not being thankful to God. He counted his blessings every day. One day as he sat by the fire and read his Bible, he asked the family to all come in and sit with him. After they were all gathered around—all seven of them—he said, "I just want to take this time to thank Jesus. Do you realize April and I have survived the enemy in Iraq and Afghanistan? And that we all have survived the Islamic terrorist attacks, the ISIS attacks, the gangs, and even the elements? Satan has attacked with all he has, but we have survived. I want us to pause and thank God."

The family looked a little sheepish as they realized what Jerry said was true, and they had kind of taken it all for granted. For the first time in several weeks, the prayer time was truly meaningful to them.

EIGHTEEN

Industry Makes a Comeback

GM, Ford, and Chrysler had all started factories once again down in rural Alabama and middle Tennessee. Whole new towns had sprung up in just a few months. These companies had purchased equipment from Canada and Germany. Toyota had moved their production back to Japan. But anyone who wanted a job could get one if they wanted to move, yet only two or three families from the Crossroads area decided to go.

The government had actually broken up the EPA. Their very rigid rules no longer applied. The automobiles and trucks being turned out could use the standards established in the early 1990s. Not many people could purchase new autos or trucks right now, but the prices were many thousands of dollars less than the last models produced.

As a matter of fact, wages and prices were lower everywhere. The dollar was worth what it had been in the early 1900s. People were cautious with their money. Many people had lost thousands of dollars in property and cash, though at this point, almost everyone was in the same boat.

These survivors were learning to live smarter and were far more conservative and creative than they had been just three years before. Yes indeed, America would survive and come back stronger than ever.

Spring, Year Four

In late March, the weather began to break. It was too early to plow but they had time on their hands. Jerry confided in April that he thought they needed to explore west of them toward Denver. He wanted to find out something about Rachael's family if possible.

That night after the boys were in bed, Jerry and April asked Rachael to stay up and talk with them. Jerry began the conversation, "How would you feel about going toward Denver to see if we can find out anything about your family?"

Rachael smiled as she had not smiled in several weeks. "Oh yes, can we please?"

They made plans to leave as soon as they could. April agreed that she and the boys would keep baby Faith while Jerry, Ned, and Rachael made the journey west.

The Reunion

On a Monday morning a few days later, the Yukon was loaded with supplies, a tent, and three sleeping bags. Jerry told April they would try to be back within two weeks. He had no idea what they would run into along the way. He was very thankful now for the Road Atlas even if it was out of date. He had also borrowed a reliable compass just in case.

After a family prayer circle and a hardy breakfast of eggs, homemade biscuits, and grits, they loaded up and set out. Rachael was able to give directions for the first twenty miles, and then she became a little confused. Jerry assured her it was all right.

Using the compass, the road map, and some dead reckoning, he found a main road with a sign that indicated he was going in the right direction. At Fort Morgan, they got directions and were told they were on the right road. At Wiggins, they took a road that went south. The closer they got to Denver, the more devastation they observed. Finally, they were forced to stop and camp for the night. Rachael said her home had been near Sedalia, Colorado, just south of Denver.

The next morning after a light breakfast of fruit and flatbread, they continued south. After a few more miles, they noticed there was not as much damage as there had been farther north. They noticed more people, and most of the homes appeared to be occupied.

Suddenly at a small, unnamed crossroad community, Rachael said, "Stop, I know this place!" She told Jerry to turn right. After three or four miles, she said, "Turn left at the next road." Rachael's breathing was getting faster. Jerry guessed her heart was about to beat out of her chest. "There it is! That's my house!"

Jerry stopped the Yukon, turned to her and said, "Rachael, don't get your hopes too high." He slowly turned into the concrete driveway and stopped. Rachael beat both Ned and Jerry to the front door.

The next sound anyone heard was, "Oh my God, you are alive!" It was the voice of an older woman, who had appeared in the doorway. She took Rachael in her arms, their bodies wrapped together so closely they appeared to be one. The woman had straggly, gray hair and a dress that hung on her bony frame. Jerry could tell she had once been a larger woman who had lost weight. By this time, he and Ned felt like they were intruders on a scene from a movie.

Rachael suddenly remembered Jerry and Ned. She quickly made the introductions. Ruth Byrd led everyone into an unadorned living area. Rachael asked about her father and her brother. Ruth broke down and began to sob. Through the sobs, she said Rachael's brother Robbie was missing and presumed dead. Ruth then led them into a bedroom just off the living room.

In a queen-sized bed lay an emaciated figure that

looked more like a skeleton than a man. He had been a tall man, but he looked almost infant-like in that large bed. Most of his hair was gone and his complexion was a pale shade of gray. His eyes seemed to bulge out of his skull. He rasped in a weak voice, "Rachael, my baby girl, come here; please, baby, come here."

Jerry led Ned out of the room. This homecoming was too personal for strangers to be gawking. Jerry went to the kitchen and looked in the refrigerator. Nothing but a quart carton of milk, nearly empty. In the cabinet was a half loaf of bread, a can of pork and beans, and a few crackers. That was all. This family was starving.

After about fifteen minutes, Jerry went back into the bedroom, Ned following close on his heels, and checked in on the reunited family. From what he could tell, the man was very sick with either radiation sickness or cancer.

He and Ned went to the Yukon and unloaded all the food they had with them, except for some of the flatbread and a can of fruit. He put it all in the refrigerator for safekeeping.

Jerry and Ned planned to sleep in the Yukon that night, while Rachael would sleep with her mother in the house. Actually, neither of ladies would sleep much that night; Robert Byrd needed attention every few minutes.

Rachael's mother said a doctor was supposed to come around in the morning with some more medicine for him. Before Jerry and Ned went to the vehicle to sleep, Jerry knelt beside the bed, took the bony hand of Rachael's dad in his, and prayed that God would relieve him.

Before the sun came up God answered that prayer, and Robert Byrd was released from this world. He had gotten to see his baby girl one last time.

When the doctor came the next morning, he wrote out a death certificate and gave Ruth some pills that she was supposed to take every day for her own condition. Then in a very matter-of-fact fashion, he told Ruth that he would send someone for the body of her husband. Jerry was surprised to learn that funerals were not the norm in this part of the country—when people died, they were simply buried as soon as possible. On the last day of the month, a memorial was held in the chapel of the local funeral home for all who had died in that month.

It sounded so cold to Jerry, but he could see that this was out of necessity to keep disease at a minimum and to expedite matters. He was glad they did things differently back at the Crossroads.

Later that day two men dressed in white jumpsuits came in a van for the body. Jerry took Ruth and Rachael out of the room and into the backyard while the body was being placed in a body bag and loaded into the van. There, Jerry prayed for them.

The next morning Jerry asked Ruth and Rachael what they wanted to do. He said it might not be safe to stay there, as no one seemed to know for sure how bad the fallout had been. Ruth was sick herself, but was it radiation sickness or some secondary disease caused by the polluted atmosphere? No matter. Jerry invited Ruth to go back with them, but she insisted that she wanted to stay at her home. Rachael said she needed to get back to her baby, but would make a decision later.

The food Jerry took into the house would last Ruth a few days until they could make a return trip with more supplies for her.

Later that morning, Jerry, Ned, and Rachael made a quick, uneventful trip back to Shockley's Crossroads.

Jerry put the word out that Rachael's mother needed some supplies. By noon the next day, there was more food, blankets, clothing and over-the-counter medicine than would fit in the Yukon. The cabinetmaker had a covered utility trailer, and he told Jerry to load it down and take it. This way, when they made the trip back to Sedalia, the whole family could go.

Four adults, two young boys, and a baby loaded in the Yukon and made the trip. This time it took six hours. When they arrived, they found that Ruth looked much better than when they had seen her last. She was rested, had eaten well, and had taken her medication. She wore a fresh dress, and her hair was brushed. Rachael was clearly pleased to see her mother looking better.

When Rachael introduced Ruth to her new granddaughter, Ruth was overjoyed, tears streaming down her face as she looked the child in her arms. She told Rachael she was so glad she chose to keep the baby and that she loved the name. She kept whispering it to her, "Faith, Faith, my beautiful little Faith."

When Ruth saw all the food and supplies, she started weeping again, this time overwhelmed by the generosity of others. She insisted on sharing some of her good fortune with a couple of neighbors, which made Jerry smile. He told her they would try to check on her once a month, so she should keep a running list of things that she needed.

NINETEEN

Seed Time

As early May rolled around, it was time to plow, disk, and plant in northeast Colorado. The family planted the May peas, cabbage, radishes, and potatoes first. Next, they planted the field corn and string beans. The tomatoes Jerry had started from seed in the house behind the woodstove were planted in mid-June. He waited for God to work his miracle of making all the things grow. And grow they did.

Rain came at just the right times. The summer was not too hot. And when fall came, there was even more food stored for the winter, and more food to share with the less fortunate and the elderly who could not raise their own gardens.

One Sunday at the church building, Jerry asked the people who were present—this particular Sunday the attendance had increased to fifty-five people—if they thought it would be possible to start a food pantry for those who got in a bind. No one disputed that this would be a good thing.

From then on, with every first Sunday of the month, people would bring canned goods and even some fresh vegetables to church. A corner at the back of the building was made into a storeroom, complete with shelves and bins for fresh vegetables. The people who attended could help themselves if they needed anything. Some just traded one kind of canned goods or fresh vegetable for another. The pantry was a huge success.

Every other month, Jerry loaded up the Yukon and took a load of goods to Rachael's mother over in Sedalia. She, in turn, shared with others who were in need.

Ruth's health had improved quite a bit with the good food, rest, and proper medication. Rachael and Faith usually made the trip to see her mother. But Rachael did not offer to move back in with her mother. And Ruth didn't want to leave her home.

Questions Answered

Jerry had always been an inquisitive man. He tried to find out what happened to the countries who had attacked the United States. Finally, through the representatives who were sent to Charlotte, NC, he learned that Iran had tried to send nuclear missiles to Israel at the same time America was being attacked. But Israel had been alert. It had not been asleep at the wheel. Its anti-ballistic missiles had taken out the warhead rockets before they got over Israel. These had exploded and killed many Iranians.

Israel did not stop there. It then sent long-range bombers over North Korea and cut the head off the serpent. At the same time, it warned Russia and China to stay out of the conflict or face the consequences. Israel froze these two giant nations in their tracks. All of Israel's citizens were armed and hunkered down, ready to defend their nation. The army and air force were ready for any secondary attack that might come. No other attacks were mounted.

All of American military in foreign lands were ordered to begin to leave their military bases as soon as President Ryan assumed his office. Armed Forces stationed in Germany, Japan, South Korea, the Philippines, Great Britain, and all around the world began to pack up and return to the US.

They mainly came into the port cities along the Gulf Coast. When they got to the mainland, they were to assume border security, start clean-up operations, restore communication lines, and provide transportation where needed. This, of course, took some time simply because of the logistics of such a large operation.

Within two years, America took on the look of a giant

fort with all weapons pointed toward her borders. It would be a very long time before the America would again fall victim to a surprise attack.

The Army Corps of Engineers supervised the rebuilding and repairing of bridges, roads, and even some buildings. There would be no price gouging or cost overruns while they were in charge.

Steel mills that had been closed for many years were repaired and reopened. Iron ore and junk cars began to be hauled by freight train and trucks to these factories. Many thousands of tons of steel would be needed.

Forests that had been protected by the EPA and the Department of the Interior were invaded and clear-cut for lumber that was so badly needed. As soon as the trees were cut and cleared, young people were recruited and paid by the large timber companies to replant seedlings. Lumber would be needed for many years down the road.

No one except the truly certified disabled were assisted by the federal government without working. Any assistance was mainly in the form of food, housing, and utilities. People who were physically able still drew some welfare money but they had to work at least forty hours a week for the federal or local government in order to draw it. The work they were required to do was manual labor, clearing towns and cities of rubble as long as it was safe to do so.

After a few months of this kind of labor, many of the people found work that was more profitable in the private sector at GM, Ford, and Chrysler. Others went to work in the construction business, building homes and factories. America was on her way back from the ruins. The days of the free handout had ended abruptly. Ironically, the very people who hated capitalism had actually strengthened capitalism by their cowardly attack.

Back at Shockley's Crossroads, people began to receive their electric bill once again. But the rates were ridiculously low. A typical electric bill was twelve to fifteen dollars. The people didn't complain and gladly paid it. The American dollar was quite deflated.

People were saving their money again, but they were not putting it in the bank or buying stocks. They were hiding their money, at least at first. President Ryan eventually asked the Federal Reserve to increase the interest rate on money. After a few months, this helped. People began to open savings accounts. Trust in government was slowly returning.

One day a local farmer came driving up to the Crossroads in a brand new Ford F-150 truck. He had been able to swing a loan and bought it for sixty-five hundred dollars. It was not long before others who could afford it were driving new Chevys, Fords, and Dodge trucks and SUVs. Inexpensive transportation was just what the doctor ordered to get America back on its feet.

The oil and gas business began to boom once again. With new vehicles being sold, gas and oil would be needed. A gallon of gas was forty-nine cents, which was more than gas was in the early 1900s. But still, it was cheap, and it all came from American oil wells.

Jerry's old Yukon just kept on running. He changed the oil and put new spark plugs in it. He changed the fluid and filter in the transmission and eventually had to find some better tires. The seats were worn, the headliner was coming down in places, but it just kept on running. In his spare time, he built a utility trailer so he could carry more supplies to Sedalia.

———

Jerry's heart was still heavy, though, because on Sunday mornings, the old church building, which they now called Christ's Church at Raccoon Creek, was never more than about a third full. The empty pews bothered Jerry a lot.

He wanted to see more people express their gratefulness for their good fortunes by joining with others in worship at the local church. He began to make rounds once a week to homes of people who had never come to church. He talked with them about Jesus. Some listened. Some acted bored. A few became agitated. But he never gave up.

The Sermon

One morning, Jerry received a call on his fire department radio about an emergency at Shockley's Crossroads. When he arrived, one of the militiamen was frantically giving Frank Shockley CPR. This went on for a good forty-five minutes with different people taking turns. There was no hospital or doctor close by. Old Doc Tom was thirty miles away. Finally, Major Charles Stewart stepped up and put his hand on the shoulder of the man giving CPR. He said, "It's over, friend. He's gone." Grown men began to weep. One of the best and most loyal friends the Crossroads had was dead from a massive heart attack. No power on earth could keep him from dying. He was now in the arms of God.

Jerry knew one other thing for certain: there at the Crossroads, no one was going to come take the body away in a body bag and dump it in a hole. No sir, that was not the way it would be done in their community.

As the women comforted Thelma Shockley, four men wrapped Frank in a blanket and gently carried him into the store and laid his body on the counter. The cabinetmaker told Thelma he would be bringing a casket that afternoon.

Jerry asked her if he could hold a funeral at Christ's Church for this fine man. Through sobs, she nodded.

That afternoon the cabinetmaker delivered the most

beautiful wooden coffin Jerry had ever seen. It was made from polished cherry wood and lined with a beautiful, light-blue linen sheet with a matching pillow for his head. Jerry learned that the cabinetmaker had built this coffin for himself. But out of love, he provided it for his friend. It reminded Jerry of the borrowed tomb provided for Jesus by Joseph of Arimathea in John 19:38.

People came by the store all that evening and into the night to pay their respects. It was announced that the funeral would be at the Raccoon Creek Church the next morning at eleven o'clock.

By ten thirty the next morning the church building was full, and by eleven o'clock people were standing around the walls. A few folks were standing outside.

Jerry thought to himself, "It's a shame it took this to fill the old building." There was singing of the old hymns, which April led. Surprisingly, the singing was really good. Deacon Wallace read some scripture and had a prayer that lasted way too long.

Then Jerry came to the pulpit, opened his Bible, read Psalm 23 and John 14:1-6. Then he closed his Bible and preached his heart out. He reminded the people that anyone of them could also be called away at any moment. One did not have to be old to die. And no one gets to heaven except through Jesus Christ. It was as Jesus said in that sixth verse, "No one comes to the father except through me." One last verse of "In the Garden" was sung by the congregation before the people filed slowly out of the building.

The pallbearers carried the beautiful, cherry coffin into the churchyard where it was placed above the open grave that had been prepared. There under the branches of an old oak tree, Frank Shockley's body would lie until the great resurrection day. Jerry contemplated to himself that the branches of that tree reminded him of two open arms. April, Ned, and Rachael sang "Amazing Grace" a cappella. Jerry ended the service with a short prayer.

He hoped the message had hit a nerve with the crowd. But he had no idea. He thought to himself, "Time will tell. It always does."

The funeral service had made more of an impression than Jerry could have imagined. The next Sunday morning at eleven o'clock, the building was about three-quarters full. And for the next several Sundays, even more people began to attend. The messages were simple, and people found that Jerry had a way of illustrating how God works in the lives of those who love Him and are obedient to Him.

In the next few months, the old stock watering tank got a workout. Almost every week, people were coming forward at the invitation time. God was blessing the people, and they were becoming aware of His blessings.

———

Love Never Fails

From the first day Rachael had come to live with the Hunt family, Ned had his eye on her. Unbeknown to him, she also had her eye on Ned.

Rachael was almost two years older than Ned, but emotionally they were the same age. There were very few people their age in the Crossroads community. Such a situation could present a problem when an unrelated couple live in the same house. The Hunts had handled it well. But it was natural for Ned and Rachael to be attracted to each other.

Ned also was very kind and helpful with baby Faith. Some evenings with little to do, the couple sat on the porch and shared their dreams. They just talked about what they would like to be or do in the future.

One evening as they sat in the porch swing with Faith between them, Ned said he supposed he needed to learn a trade, because for the next ten or twenty years there was going to be a lot of construction and rebuilding in America. Rachael said, "I used to want to become a doctor like my dad." Then she added, "But now all I want to do is raise my little girl."

Out of the clear blue, Ned said, "I want to help raise her

with you." Rachael took Ned's hand, pulled him toward her, and lightly kissed him on the lips.

It was now out in the open. The fire had been ignited. Love was in full bloom. Ned said, "We have to tell April and Jerry how we feel. Let's tell them as soon as Faith is in bed."

About ten o'clock that evening Ned and Rachael walked into the living room holding hands. Jerry was reading a book, and April was knitting. As the Hunts looked up, they immediately noticed the young couple holding hands. Jerry said, "What is it?"

Ned blurted out, "We want to get married!"

April showed no surprise at all, while Jerry, who was normally quite astute, seemed taken back by the statement. He made a rather dumb comment: "To each other?" Everyone laughed except Jerry.

April then said, "Well, duh, silly, of course to each other." She arose from her chair and hugged them both. Jerry sat with his mouth open . . . but silent.

Now this was another first for the Crossroads community. There had not been a wedding at Shockley's Crossroads in four or five years. Since the attack and government agencies had been disrupted, a question arose: what do people need to do to become legally married?

This was a question for Senator Charles Stewart or

perhaps Congressman Doug Phillips, who had been appointed to replace Frank Shockley.

Jerry sent a message by a courier to the "Major" as everyone still called him. The message gave the circumstances and asked what they could do.

The Major made a special trip to the Crossroads the next weekend. He said licenses, permits, and certificates were being issued from the state office building that had been set up in Colorado Springs. The couple would be issued a marriage license if they made an appearance there. Also, since Jerry was holding religious services, he would be recognized as a legal officiant for weddings.

On Tuesday of the next week, the Hunts, along with Ned Carney and Rachael Byrd, made an appearance at the Register of Deeds office in Colorado Springs. They answered a few questions, filled out two simple forms, and were approved. The couple could be married, and Jerry could legally marry them or anyone else in the State of Colorado. The era of "red tape" was over.

TWENTY

Senator (Major) Stewart and Representative Doug Phillips came back to the Crossroads every weekend unless they were in a specially called session. They helped make laws but were also willing to live under the laws they made. Their salaries were meager.

The new lawmakers had insisted that their salaries must be in line with what the people made. The mean income in Colorado was calculated to be just under fifteen thousand dollars a year, two years after the attack. And so, the salaries were set at sixteen thousand for senators and fifteen thousand for representatives. They were allowed five hundred dollars per year for travel expenses.

Injured but dangerous

The second year after the attack, security was relaxed. Some militia groups were all but disbanded. Several hundred cells of terrorists had been arrested and were being held in federal prisons. Some had been tried by military tribunals and dozens had been executed. The danger appeared to be over.

However, Muslim terrorists were a patient crew. Many had escaped detection and had slithered into the shadows like cockroaches hiding in the darkness.

Late Spring

Memorial Weekend was set aside by the Hunt family to host a large wedding. The whole Shockley's Crossroads community was invited to the Carney and Byrd wedding. It was to be a gala event.

The Raccoon Creek Church building was decorated by a committee of ladies who had not been a part of a wedding in too many years. They were excited. There were flowers and greenery. The cabinetmaker had constructed an arch on the stage and painted it white. There were four candlesticks complete with five, long, white candles on each of the candlesticks. Yes indeed, it was going to be a wedding to remember.

A rehearsal was held on Friday evening with an old-fashioned rehearsal supper to follow for the wedding party and family. Lon and John would stand up with Ned, and April was the Matron of Honor.

Senator Stewart and Representative Phillips came in that weekend with plans to attend the wedding. Since they were honored guests, they were invited to the rehearsal dinner at the Hunt house. Their wives were unable to attend due to prior commitments.

It was about eight thirty, and dessert with coffee had just been served, when two pickup trucks came sliding into the driveway. Four militiamen came rushing toward the porch. When Jerry opened the door, he saw that their faces were white as sheets . . . and one had blood on his sleeve.

They all tried to talk at once. Finally, one took control and said there had been a horrible shooting at two homes in the community. The senator's house and the congressman's house. They were needed at once.

Jerry followed Senator Stewart to his house while Ned and two other men went to Representative Phillips' house.

It was really bad news at both homes. Georgia Stewart was dead. She had been shot several times. No one else was home, but the house had been ransacked. It was obvious they had been looking for the senator.

At Doug Phillips' house, it was the same story . . . only worse. His wife and daughter were dead. They had suffered multiple gunshot wounds. His daughter's boyfriend, Fred Morgan, was seriously wounded, but it appeared he would survive. Jerry took it upon himself to dispatch someone to fetch Doc Tom from Silver Lode.

There had also been trouble at Shockley's store. It had been riddled with large caliber bullets from some sort of automatic weapon. Thelma had been in the store at the time, but had thrown herself down behind the counter and pretended to be dead. She gave a description of the four men who shot up the place. It was the same description Fred Morgan had given. They had spoken broken English and had shouted, "Allah is God, Allah is great."

The state police were notified. Three hours later a team of investigators arrived. They told of other attacks around the state and in other states as well. These attacks were mainly on government officials.

Stewart and Phillips had escaped only because they were not where they were expected to be. Stewart, being the military man he was, laid aside his grief, and took off his senator's hat for a moment.

He was standing ramrod straight as he jutted out his jaw and said, "The militia has got to become more proactive." He looked straight at Jerry and said, "I am appointing you to head up the militia here in my absence. This must never happen again in our county."

Jerry stiffened, saluted, and said, "Yes sir, I will get right on this."

Doug Phillips was still in a state of shock over the death of his wife and only daughter.

There was no wedding the next day. There were two funerals instead. Mrs. Stewart's funeral was at eleven o'clock and was over by twelve-fifteen as ordered by the Major. By one o'clock, that grave had been filled.

At precisely two o'clock in the afternoon, Jerry stepped

to the pulpit again. This time there were two rough-wooden coffins in front of the podium. But again, just as at the eleven o'clock service, the building was full. Four militiamen again stood guard near the road. There would be no sneak attack this day.

Jerry mentioned each lady and offered words of comfort to the family as he read scripture and delivered a short message. By four thirty, three mounds of fresh dirt represented the three lives, people who had made a difference to those around them. He stood in the churchyard a long time after everyone had left.

Jerry observed four graves for people that he had only known a few short years, but had learned to love. He lifted a silent prayer to God. He asked God to put an end to this madness. He also asked God for strength to take on the new responsibilities that had been thrust upon him.

In his heart, he wondered about the compatibility of these jobs: husband, father, preacher, and commander of a militia unit. A weapon in one hand, a Bible in the other. Then he remembered what he had read about the American Revolution when the nation was in the process of being born. Many preachers were also soldiers.

Finally, on the way back to the farmhouse, he remembered the talk he had with God that very first day of the attack. "Just me and you, God . . . can save my family," he had said. He and God had done very well so far in saving his family and even some strangers along the way.

Just before bedtime that night Jerry asked God for the strength, wisdom, and courage to do all the things he had to do. And then he added. "Thank you, God, for you must have the glory, not me. Amen."

Jerry awoke in a sweat about 0300 hours on Wednesday morning of the next week. He had an epiphany that had shaken him badly. The men who planned and carried out the attacks on the families of Senator Stewart and Representative Phillips knew they had failed in assassinating them. "They will try again," Jerry muttered to himself.

This could be their undoing. This could be the best way to catch these terrorists—when they try again. When Stewart and Phillips were away from home, they were constantly surrounded by police and bodyguards. However, the guard had been relaxed when these two men were home.

Limited cell phone service was in use once again. Service came and went, and the signal was not always good. But it was better than nothing. Jerry called Senator Stewart and told him the next time he and Representative Phillips were home, he wanted to have a meeting with them.

A phone call from Stewart Thursday night told Jerry that both he and Phillips would be home Saturday morning very early. Jerry asked them both to come to his house for a breakfast meeting around 0900 hours.

Stewart and Phillips arrived precisely at 0900 hours with Charles Stewart driving. Two stern-looking men in cheap suits sat in the backseat. They cautiously exited the car, looking all around, and then opened the doors for their charges. Stewart had his steely-eyed, square-jaw look as always. Jerry thought, "He would be a heck of a poker player." Doug Phillips looked pale and haggard, almost sick. He was taking the death of his wife and daughter very hard.

After a scrumptious meal of scrambled eggs, bacon, grits, and homemade biscuits washed down with coffee, April excused herself. Jerry cleared the table and laid out his plan.

Both of them would be under constant surveillance from the time they left the government building until they returned. The best men in the militia had volunteered to provide the additional cover. The bodyguards would still be provided by the state police as basic protection. What the militiamen were providing was just extra. They probably would not even know these men were close by.

Both men agreed this was a good plan. Just as the meeting was concluding, Jerry went to the foot of the stairs and called out, "Come on down." Two men came lumbering down from upstairs where they had been concealed and on lookout. Two more men came from the back porch where they had been lying in wait.

The plan was already in place. There were some twelve men who would be taking shifts each weekend. They were well-armed with side arms and an AR-15 each. Jerry had already started training them. He had not survived in Iraq and Afghanistan by being unprepared.

Each week he would upgrade their training. He would be giving more pointers on picking out the bad guys and keeping these essential men safe.

At the same time, the plan was this: when these interlopers showed back up, they would be exterminated like vermin.

The second of July dawned warm and dry. Just two more days until the wedding that had been postponed. The community had mourned the tragic assault of the Stewart and Phillips residences for more than thirty days. It was time to move along.

Plans were back in place, and the decorations were back up. There would be a short rehearsal on Thursday evening with just a few people involved. They had gone through the rehearsal before.

The wedding was set for the Fourth of July with a

huge barbecue to follow. This would be a Colorado-type barbeque with beef roasted on a grill built into the ground. The beef would be started at about 0400 hours and would be done at about 1600 hours. It would be roasted nice and slow by four guys who knew what to do with charcoal and beef.

At two o'clock in the afternoon, the ceremony was begun in the Raccoon Creek Church building. Rachael was a beautiful bride, and Ned never looked more handsome. This time the wedding went exactly as planned.

The reception was at the Hunt home in the yard. Sawhorse tables with white sheets for tablecloths were lined up in the yard. The shade trees and the porch were reserved for the wedding party and the older folks.

By six o'clock that evening, there was not much left of that beef and everyone appeared to be enjoying themselves to the fullest.

It was soon time to send off the young couple.

Senator Stewart had offered his house to them for the weekend. He was going to stay with Representative Phillips. They both needed some company and this filled the bill. Faith went home with Jerry and April.

The rest of the weekend and the next week were uneventful. The garden needed attention and minor repairs were needed at the Hunt home and at the church building.

Senator Stewart said he wanted Ned, Rachael, and Faith to stay in his house full-time. When Senator Stewart was home on weekends, he would sleep in the guestroom. It was a comfortable room with an attached bath. He had a table and chair for writing, and a nice leather recliner for his reading. It was all he needed.

Ned, Rachael, and baby Faith still showed up almost every evening for supper with the Hunt family. That was fine with the Hunts; they kind of missed them when they were gone. Poor Thor didn't want to leave his home with the Hunts. He spent as much time with Lon and Jon as he did with Ned. One was just as apt to find Thor at the Hunt house as with Ned.

Ned came down twice a week and worked in the garden. He also showed up at all the militia meetings, which had started up once again on Wednesday night and half a day on Saturday. Rachael often came to the house with Ned.

Lon and Jon had really matured in the last five years. Lon was seventeen, Jon was fifteen, and so they came to all the militia meetings as well. They could not be full-fledged Stewart's Rangers until they turned eighteen. But it was amazing how much they had picked up. They had also become proficient with all the weapons. As the saying goes, "They knew the drill."

Weeks had now gone by since the horrible attack on the homes of Stewart and Phillips. It was somewhat like waiting for the other shoe to drop. These radicals would not give up; Jerry could just feel it. It was just a question of when and how they would make their move. Men like Senator Stewart and Representative Phillips were so much like the Founding Fathers that no enemy of the US could let them govern successfully.

Hundreds of leaders had emerged from the ashes, and America was rebounding even faster than anticipated. After a disaster and in the midst of crisis, Americans have always arisen to the occasion. This was no exception.

TWENTY ONE

Late one Sunday night all of the Carney family were asleep. Thor was sleeping at the foot of the bed in Ned and Rachael's bedroom. Faith was on her cot in the corner of the room.

Thor suddenly rose to his feet, laid back his ears, and growled low in his throat. Ned turned on a flashlight he kept on the nightstand and reached for his 1911 .45 caliber pistol. With the flashlight in his left hand and the 1911 in his right, he rolled out of bed and eyeballed Thor.

Something was wrong.

Ned shook Rachael and pushed her toward the edge of the bed. He whispered for her to get the baby and crawl to the closet. They had practiced this drill more than a few times.

He commanded Thor to stay at the bedroom door while he crept down the stairs. Then he heard the low rumble of several muffled motorcycles. At the foot of the stairs, he knocked softly on the senator's door.

The senator was already up and had an AR-15 along with four extra magazines of ammo in his hands. He posted himself at the front door while Ned went to the back door.

Near the door in a corner was propped a 12-gauge pump-action shotgun. He knew it was fully loaded with heavy shot.

It sounded like there were two or three motorcycles. Then they went silent. The night was full darkness, as the moon had already slid below the horizon. But at all four corners of the house were floodlights. These lights could be activated by motion or manually; however, the motion detector was turned off on purpose. There were four switches in a row that could be turned on, all at one time or individually. The senator was at these switches. As a proficient military man, he would decide when and where this battle would start.

The four, swarthy figures dressed in black dismounted their cycles. It was highly likely they had explosives. Stewart was determined they would not get in the house with them. By this time, Ned was aware that they were going to try to come in the front door. He positioned himself on the other side of the doorway. Stewart quietly released the lock on the door, twisted the knob, and motioned that he was going to fling the door open on the count of three. One … two … three … the floodlights at the front of the house were flipped on and the door flung open simultaneously. Four floodlights shined down on the faces of men in night-vision goggles; they were instantly blinded. The door was now open and the quick, sharp reports of the AR-15 and the 12-gauge were deafening.

The shots were so rapid that no one could have counted them. The element of shock and awe was drastic. There were only a couple of rounds of return fire. Ned emptied the 12-gauge, drew his .45, and fired four more shots randomly in the direction of the motorcycles.

In the meantime, Stewart replaced his empty magazine with a fully loaded one. The interior of the house was completely dark in contrast to the floodlights outside. Four bodies lay in awkward positions in pools of blood. Two were as close as six feet from the porch, one was about twelve feet away, and one was nearly twenty feet away. From the time the lights came on until the last round was fired could not have been more than forty-five seconds.

The smell of gunpowder was heavy in the air. The sound of a baby crying could eventually be heard. Faith.

Thor had obeyed and stayed at his post. No one would touch his charges as long as he had breath. He was one loyal dog.

Ned started to go out to examine the bodies, but Senator Stewart held his arm and motioned no: they could have unexploded bombs on them. These groups often did that. About as many people had been killed by dead terrorists as live ones.

But where were the bodyguards? It was learned later that they had been decoyed away fifteen minutes before the attack. But they would never fall for that trick again after Senator Stewart got through dressing them down.

Meanwhile, a few miles away another drama was in progress.

Two black-clad cyclists motored up to the Phillips home.

Doug Phillips had not slept well since his wife and daughter had been killed. He was upstairs reading at one o'clock in the morning. He heard something but was not sure what it was. Perhaps it was a motorcycle or maybe it was Ned on his dirt bike coming to bring him a message.

Nevertheless, he alertly turned off the light and started to the doorway with his AR-15 and one extra magazine of ammo. He had not yet made it to the top of the stairs when there was a loud explosion—an explosion so violent that it rattled the house, and flung him backward and to the floor. Then there was gunfire. An enormous amount of gunfire. It went on for at least a minute or two. Listening, he could tell that weapons were being reloaded at times.

Then a familiar voice shouted out to him, "Lieutenant Doug, are you all right?" It was one of the bodyguards from Stewart's Rangers.

Doug Phillips shouted back, "I'm all right. Come on up."

The voice came back, "We can't; the stairway is gone."

The explosion had been a large, homemade satchel

explosive. It had demolished the front entrance and the first eight steps of the stairway.

The would-be assassins were dead from many gunshot wounds. The bodyguards were all alive. Two had superficial wounds from shrapnel. One had a flesh wound from a bullet. Someone quickly brought a ladder and placed it so Phillips could descend to the ground floor.

There were now six bodies that needed to be identified and dispatched. The FBI crime lab would be called in as soon as the bomb squads were through with the bodies and they were rendered harmless.

The militia group took possession of the six motorcycles, one of which had become a casualty in the gunfire, so it would be cannibalized for parts. Americans had once again learned to not waste things. Very little was actually junked anymore. Repair, invent, and improvise became the motto.

TWENTY TWO

After the spring planting, Jerry felt a little restless, and since he'd long been wanting to find out what had happened to his parents in Greensboro, NC, he decided to make the trip.

But he wanted to make this trip alone.

After getting April's blessings and assurance that she and the boys would be okay on their own for a few days, he called Senator Stewart to apprise him of his plan. Stewart not only approved but offered to escort him via helicopter, as he also had business on the East Coast. It was time again to do an assessment of damages and progress. Ned and the others would handle the militia duties while they were gone.

At 0745 hours just a few days later, the *chop chop chop* of a helicopter could be heard as it descended in the pasture next to the farmhouse. The engine was cut and two figures hopped out, one of which was Stewart. The other was a slightly shorter man with a stocky build—a

Marine with sergeant stripes. Jerry already had a duffel bag packed and waiting at the front door.

Stewart introduced the sergeant as GySgt. Roland Mitchell; he was their extra protection for the trip. Stewart asked Jerry if he had his sidearm with him, which he did, in his duffle. Stewart said, "Strap it on." Jerry noted they were all packing.

After a final kiss planted on April and a hug for the boys, Jerry joined the two men and ran to the helicopter.

The pilot's name was Capt. George Cooper, and Jerry noted that he, too, was carrying a sidearm.

By 0815, Captain Cooper had lifted the Bell 206L helicopter from the ground and flew over the Crossroads, headed due east. Flying slow and low in order to observe and photograph the ground below, the aircraft took them over Colorado, Kansas, Missouri, and Illinios, and then to Indiana—Stewart had made arrangements for a hotel room near Indianapolis. They'd stopped and refueled twice along the way.

After arriving in Indianapolis, they were whisked away, covered by additional security from the state police and National Guard, to their hotel in the town of Speedway. They enjoyed a delicious fried-chicken dinner at a local restaurant, then went straight to their rooms.

The wake-up call came at 0500, but Jerry had already been up, drunk a cup of coffee, and had his normal session with God. He was ready to roll after a light breakfast in the lobby. They headed back to the airport for another surveillance flight. The chopper had been refueled and inspected, but Captain Cooper did his own inspection as well. He walked all around the chopper, double-checking everything with a keen eye, before flipping the switch. He warmed up the engine, listening for any sounds that would indicate problems, and upon finding none, he revved it up and they lifted off.

They would fly southeast following the interstate to Cincinnati, then south to Knoxville.

Some portions of the highway were busier than others. The major bridge over the Ohio River was still out, and construction was ongoing. However, there was another bridge open and active with traffic. Near Knoxville, the roads were clogged with cars, and traffic was at a standstill. The I-40 overpasses had been hit badly in several places and not much repair had been done. Stewart noted all of this on a tape recorder as Sergeant Mitchell took pictures.

When the chopper needed fuel and evening had fallen, Captain Cooper landed at a small airport near a mountain resort. Since there did not seem to be security around, the sergeant and the captain would stay with the chopper throughout the night.

Stewart and Jerry went into the cramped terminal and got some food at the coffee shop, including hamburgers, fries, and coffee to take to Cooper and Mitchell. They learned that the Tennessee Highway Patrol would have at least two men at the airport throughout the night. Still, they decided to stick close to the chopper, sleeping in the recliners in the terminal. It was a long night.

The next morning as Jerry and the senator walked to the chopper, they noted four Tennessee State Troopers present. There had been some strange activity in the area. Some people on a couple of powerful motorcycles had driven around the perimeter of where the helicopter was parked. Two troopers gave chase, but the cycles made good their getaway on a curvy mountain road.

The flight to North Carolina was a little rough, with the updrafts and downdrafts of the mountains and poor visibility due to low-hanging clouds.

But finally, they were over North Carolina just above I-40, Jerry kept his eye to the ground—looking at areas of destruction in the more populated cities, giving directions to the captain as he flew closer to Greensboro, thinking of his family. They turned north to High Point, and then the low profile of the city that Jerry had called home after leaving the service—Greensboro—came into sight. He recognized some of the landmarks, but the city was strangely quiet. No traffic was moving. No life on the streets below.

A call came across the radio to Captain Cooper to set the chopper down in a certain area well outside the city. As the Bell 206L settled on a grassy area, a large, black Suburban escorted by two black Ford Expeditions pulled within a couple hundred feet, and a tall, middle-aged man along with two military men got out of the Suburban.

With the engine shut off, Senator Stewart, Jerry, and Sergeant Mitchell hopped out and met the other three men about halfway.

The tall gentleman was Thom Johnson, the new lieutenant governor of North Carolina. After introductions and handshakes, Senator Stewart was informed it was still too dangerous to go into the city. A very dirty H-bomb had detonated above the city on that fateful day. The city's population was practically annihilated by that one bomb.

Johnson extended his condolences to Jerry because, if his parents had been inside or even close to the city, they were almost certainly dead. Jerry felt numb. The news didn't surprise him, but still . . . he had hoped for better news. This would mean that his parents, his brother—his family—were all gone. A tsunami of grief swept over him as memories flooded his mind.

Johnson said there was a computerized accounting of all the people they had been able to identify and offered for Jerry to look at it. The records were in a library about ten miles away in Oak Ridge.

Before they left for Oak Ridge, Stewart's party was treated to a nice lunch in a small restaurant not far from where they had landed. While Stewart and the North Carolina officials conducted business and compared notes, Jerry simply walked around outside, then sat on a bench where he reminisced over his childhood and his family. He bowed his head and prayed that they had not suffered before they died.

Instead of flying to Oak Ridge, a state trooper chauffeured Jerry in one of the Ford Expeditions that afternoon. At the large library, Jerry went through the files on the computer. He found his brother's family first. Finally, he found his father and mother. All were recorded as deceased on that fateful day in August almost six years ago.

There was an account of the HAZMAT team retrieving bodies in the city with a few pictures accompanying the stories. All the bodies had been buried in eight mass graves on the outskirts of the town. Jerry would be able to visit the site where his parents and his brother were buried if he wished.

The driver whisked Jerry to the gravesite. It was a huge, mounded, grassy area with a large stone marker in the center. There, Jerry knelt and prayed.

———

Two days later the Bell 206L helicopter set down near the Hunt house in Colorado. His family and Ned's were outside awaiting his arrival. They all embraced him. As he held little Faith in his arms, April kissed him and stroked his face. April had prepared a fantastic meal to welcome him home. There was much laughter and bantering around the table that evening. Jerry was so happy to have his immediate family gathered near him.

Later that night as Jerry sat at his desk in deep thought about all of the things that had transpired in the last six years, he borrowed a line from Revelation 21:3-4. It was out of context; however, he could not help but think of it. God himself will be with them and be their God. He will wipe every tear from their eyes and there will be no more death or mourning or crying or pain, for the old order of things has passed away. Jerry repeated that last phrase aloud. "For the old order of things has passed away."

He bowed his head and praised God for this incredible journey of faith. He spoke one more prayer and hummed to himself an old church hymn that he loved so very much, "Faith is the Victory." The first and third verses of that song in particular came easily to him.

The first: "Encamped along the hills of light, ye Christian soldiers rise and press the battle ere the night shall veil the glowing skies. Against the foe in vales below, let all our strength be hurled, faith is the victory that overcomes the world."

And the third: "On every hand the foe we find drawn up in dread array; Let tents of ease be left behind, And onward to the fray; Salvation's helmet on each head, With truth all girt bout, The earth shall tremble 'neath our tread,

And echo with our shout . . . Faith is the victory! Faith is the victory! Faith is the victory! O glorious victory, that overcomes the world!"

Then in a very bold hand, Jerry penned these final words in his journal.

"The Hunt family . . . All present or accounted for."

ABOUT THE AUTHOR

Phil Emmert began his second career when he left a secure job with the Dow Chemical Company in Indiana, where he was a research assistant. At age thirty-three, he sold his little farm near Lebanon, Indiana, and enrolled in Johnson Bible College near Knoxville, Tennessee. Upon his graduation, he went into the full-time ministry, preaching in several different Christian churches and Churches of Christ. Phil has worn many hats in his seventy-eight years.

He has been an animal technician, part-time farmer, research assistant, school bus driver, substitute schoolteacher, children's social worker, and a juvenile crime prevention counselor in a county school system. All the while, he was ministering to small churches in Tennessee and North Carolina.

From all his experiences with people and especially with children, Phil became aware that young people are ignorant of American history. Therefore, at the age of seventy-seven, he began his third career: published author. He penned the WWII-era books *When War Was Heck* and *The Afterglow of War: Lessons Learned*. He then ventured in to Christian-based stories with *The Overcomers*, and now this book, *America Rebooted*.

Phil is the father of four adult children, about which he says, "They are my greatest accomplishments." He has eleven grandchildren. He also has three adult stepchildren.